About the author

Born in Cornwall in 1953, Pippa Bartolotti was a misfit at school, but a budding pianist. She blossomed at art college and became a London fashion designer of some repute.

By 1991, she had founded and managed two of her own companies, made the shift into electronics, and moved to Wales where her family would experience the joys of a country life.

Directorships of other companies followed. She took early retirement to explore different cultures and has lived in Cuba, backpacked round India, and driven a convoy of humanitarian aid from Wales, across Europe to Gaza. Whilst attempting to enter Bethlehem, she was arrested by Israeli security and imprisoned in Givon Prison, Ramla. Currently, she lives in the USA.

She became leader of Wales Green Party in 2011. From her early days as a Samaritan to a UK speaker for Amnesty International, she has consistently campaigned for the rights of the oppressed.

THE SYMMETRIES

Book 1
Poetic Symmetry

This is a work of fiction. Names, characters, businesses, places, events and incidents are either the products of the author's imagination or used in a fictitious manner. Any resemblance to actual persons, living or dead, or actual events is purely coincidental.

PIPPA BARTOLOTTI

THE SYMMETRIES

Book 1
Poetic Symmetry

Vanguard Press

VANGUARD PAPERBACK

© Copyright 2022
Pippa Bartolotti

The right of Pippa Bartolotti to be identified as the author of this work has been asserted by her in accordance with the Copyright, Designs and Patents Act 1988.

All Rights Reserved

No reproduction, copy or transmission of this publication may be made without written permission.
No paragraph of this publication may be reproduced, copied or transmitted save with the written permission of the publisher, or in accordance with the provisions of the Copyright Act 1956 (as amended).

Any person who commits any unauthorised act in relation to this publication may be liable to criminal prosecution and civil claims for damages.

A CIP catalogue record for this title is available from the British Library.

ISBN 978 1 80016 283 9

Vanguard Press is an imprint of
Pegasus Elliot MacKenzie Publishers Ltd.
www.pegasuspublishers.com

First Published in 2022

Vanguard Press
Sheraton House Castle Park
Cambridge England

Printed & Bound in Great Britain

Dedication

This book is dedicated to the monks and nuns of Tibet who have trusted me with their heartrending stories.

THE SYMMETRIES

Book 1 — Poetic Symmetry
Book 2 — Blind Symmetry
Book 3 — Elemental Symmetry

ALSO BY PIPPA BARTOLOTTI

Barbarian

Chapter 1
The Monk

He wondered if the screams were his.

He wondered if he was dead, or nearly dead, or just in a trance. Or dreaming. Yes, dreaming. Such a comfortable thought. No. Not dreaming. There was memory in this.

Not dreaming. He thought he had been dreaming once before. But it was a trick. A trick of the mind to escape the pain. It worked for a while, but he paid the price. Undreaming was the price. The desperate dawning that the dream was not a dream had been infinitely more painful than the ruptures in his tattered body. The price he paid for thinking, even for a second, that it was a dream, was a heavier weight than all the years of suffering, and he had cried when the realisation lurched into his battered psyche. That was the first and last time he had cried in that terrible place.

The pain had gone, but he could not be sure that was a good thing. The absence of pain had made him think he was dreaming, or dead, floating in a mist of timelessness, beyond happiness and sorrow, just weightlessness, space and the cosmos bearing him gently upon a comforting tide of peace. It would have been nice to be dreaming. Or dead.

The corners of the room came slowly into focus as the spinning stopped. As if in a drunken swoon, his brain leered inwardly as his stomach lurched. A pair of brown boots came hazily into sight, then left.

He was hanging from his feet, upside down. He thought he was upside down. He thought the light came from somewhere which was not above his head. His feet. Maybe the light was leaking from his feet. It was all blurred, untrustworthy. A surreal trickery of shocks, and screaming, and silence.

And smells. The dread smell of fear. Uncompromising, acrid, inescapable fear. The metallic taste of fear, of himself, his body, his sweat and blood, exacerbated the pervading dread. His body emitting toxic pheromones of desperation and warning. Metallic, putrescent, necrogenic. And urine, and faeces, washing clumsily down his body, or rather up his upturned body. He could feel the unwanted lumping of slushy warm brown running down his back. The stench was constant, retching, sickening. The urine dripped towards his mouth, but he didn't mind. It was the pain of urination that increased the purgatory of torture. He would rather not have done it. Beatings, electric shocks, blisters and sores. Urination had become the most dreaded trial of his life.

How long had he been like this?

He thought his arm had stopped twitching, which could be a good thing, or maybe a bad thing. He concentrated on his arm. It made him feel a little bit alive. Alive was a thought. A thought might mean he was alive. Was it good to be alive? It was foolish to think in terms of what might be good, and what might be bad, because it was all bad, but in his head, he could still find good. He knew it was there, swooning over his thoughts like a gently sleeping baby, washing him from within. Good thoughts, even now, almost passive thoughts, even now, almost a smile on his face, yes, even now.

And then, the still surprising sudden shock of frozen water hitting his bare skin. No longer the icy daggers of pain, for pain was drifting out of his reach. Curious that the body still recoiled in remembered horror, detached as it was from his barely conscious mind. He thought he was meditating, he thought he was inwardly reciting the mantras he had so painstakingly learned. Top of the class he had been in the monastery. He shouldn't be proud, but it had seemed a great honour at the time. He thought he was meditating, but that scream might have been his. Involuntary, like the recoiling shock of a bucket of frozen water thrown at a numbed and naked body.

He'd lost count of the years, but he would always remember the boots. The brown ones. Shiny and new. They always looked new. As if a brand-new pair were worn every day. It was always the water with this one.

The waterboarding, the soakings, the freezings, the dripping… always the water. They were there now, those brown boots. Why brown when everyone else wore black?

"Cut him down," came the guttural, but mildly disinterested order. It was in Chinese, and though Tashi understood very little of the neighbouring tonal language, he understood those words. The long-remembered pattern of beatings, torture, electric shocks and deprivation, then when he had found a comforting place beyond endurance, the brutal release. He braced himself for the drop, turning his head to one side as his stiffened body plunged the two feet or so to the hard, concrete floor and attempted a lumpy, impossible, roll.

Strange how the body tries to keep itself alive, even when there is no actual living to be done.

He tried again to relax, to curl up and protect what he could of his shattered body, for the kicking was inevitable when the brown boots were around. Always the same places. The genitals, the kidneys, the head. He rocked to the rhythm of blows, tried to find a melody to roll with the beat of boot against body because not to roll was to break, and something in him, possibly the primal instinct to survive, or maybe it was that peculiar, ingrained love of his, was too strong to give in.

Yes, years. He had been there for years, though it was hard to know how many. Sometimes they would forget about him, and he just ate the meagre rations, and rocked, and chanted in near silence, renewing his vows, reviewing the great teachings of the Buddha, his lips moving rhythmically through the imagined books as they appeared in his mind, mentally turning the thin parchment pages of the holy texts, until the days became weeks became years, and the boy turned into a man in the dim dank cells of Drapchi prison with barely a soul to commune with.

Sometimes, when the beatings had paused, and he allowed himself the strength to muse, he would think about the others, those who had been arrested with him that day in Lhasa, the day of the Dalai Lama's birthday, the day he had said the forbidden words out loud. His young friend, just fourteen years old, standing happily beside him, outside the Potala Palace, basking in the loving sunshine, not understanding that just four words would lead to a death sentence.

"Happy birthday, Dalai Lama!" Tashi had shouted joyfully as they spilled out of the monastery onto the streets. It was such an easy thing to say, and once he had said it, he said it again, and again, for the city was full of joy and happy sunshine that day in July 1988, when he was just fifteen years old.

Yes, he remembered the neatly paved streets, the red of the robes, the colourful shops. He remembered the bright clear sky and the looming beauty of the Potala Palace. For a moment all was pure happiness.

Then the shots, the screams, the confusion. The running here, or there, or anywhere, and the panic rising in him, too slowly. As he looked around the streets were almost empty, and still he carried the forbidden photograph in his hand. Too slow. Too trusting. Too open. Too innocent. Too honest.

He didn't see it coming, but it came anyway. Wielded with venomous force, a long metal rod crashed down on him from behind. It would have killed a weaker man.

There was no court, no trial, no formal sentence, just stone walls and a small barred window. He occasionally reflected on the fact that he was not alone, that for over seventy years his fellow Buddhists had been viciously persecuted in this high homeland of Tibet.

Tashi's secluded life in a distant monastery had not embraced the enormity of what those four words could mean for an individual. The pain, the suffering, the rapes, the bloodshed of hundreds of thousands, the exiles, the spiritual torment, were barely a concept, cushioned as they were by the pervading humaneness and kindness of all he met in the monastery. Now he was living the vicious alternative reality meted out by the occupying power of China, and he clung to the thought that through this actual bodily suffering he could find wisdom, and just maybe — although it was too much to hope — the suffering and the wisdom might bring enlightenment. And thus, he took his blows, and prayed his prayers, and forgave his persecutors, and took refuge in his beliefs, and lived on despite everything in his path screaming betrayal.

Chapter 2
Tibet Falls

By 1950, Britain had grown weary of supporting Tibet. Its strategic importance as a buffer zone between the USSR and British India was nullified by the independence of the latter, and Britain, in yet another of its selfish acts of colonialism, capitulated to Chinese demands, quietly gave Tibet away — as if it was Britain's to give.

It was an act of moral cowardice. Tibet had never been a nation state in the accepted form. It did not have an army, it had not raped its land for resources. It had not poisoned the air or polluted its soil. It was a free and independent country and it had bothered no one. A place of stunning beauty and a treasure trove of natural resources, Tibet represented to a hungry and ambitious China the glaciers, the water supply, the copper, lithium, gold and silver — forever untouched, because the land and rivers were beautifully sacred, and the gentle Tibetans would never disturb it.

"The opiate of the people." That's what Chairman Mao had said when he was asked about religion. It was a phrase which until his internment had made very little impression on Tashi, yet it was this seemingly innocuous phrase which had caused the torture and death of more than a million Tibetans.

On better days, sitting cross-legged in his cell, the remaining tatters of his robes tucked around him, he would ponder the issue, for it had only recently dawned on him that the Chinese considered Buddhism to be a religion. He had not particularly indulged himself in philosophical journeys of the mind. It was not his strength. Deep thinking was usually the burden of the higher monks.

The youngest of four children, Tashi had not shown much prowess in farming, or animal husbandry, or planting crops and harvesting them, and these were the skills his family needed. Neither had he shown interest in anything tangentially related such as carpentry, or cooking. He was always willing to do whatever his parents had asked, but he lost the yaks instead of herding them home. Unable to assess or modify the strength in his hands, he frightened the chickens and broke the eggs, and frankly, he was the very opposite of an asset to the workings and day-to-day survival of the small family farm.

Yet his smile was the sweetest thing. It was not possible to punish a boy whose heart of goodness shone through his face in the form of a wide and toothy smile. He loved his family with a passion which was palpable, and they loved him back, but there came a time when a decision about his future had to be made. His mother wept, but acquiesced. Tashi would become a monk.

His father patted his shoulders and his chest in loving abruptness. "I wish you long life and good fortune," he said, and ruffled Tashi's unruly black hair with one hand whilst passing him a bundle of wrapped bread and dried yak meat with the other. His mother cried freely, as did his brothers and his sister, as did Tashi himself. He flashed her a last disarming smile, walked towards the boundary of their tiny farm, and turned in the direction of adventure. He could not know it would be the last time he would see his beloved kin.

It is a karmic honour to have a monk in the family, and thus Tashi set off with his eldest brother in good spirits, eager to meet other young monks and begin his new life. There was no apprehension, no long goodbyes. Joining the monastery was a common occurrence for young girls and boys in the region of Amdo, isolated and sprawling across the vast eastern grasslands of old Tibet. Like every young person in the area, Tashi only wished to make his family happy.

The eastern province of Amdo had seen hard times — as if life was not hard enough on the high windswept roof of the world. The Chinese army had invaded in 1959, and out of the four thousand or so men who had lived and eked out their semi-nomadic existence in this wild place, it was reported most had been killed in the following uprising. Of the three thousand monks at the nearest monastery, two thousand had been arrested. It was never known what happened to them.

The invasion of the Chinese had been brutal. Tibet had no army. In fact, it had very little in the way of governance. Of course, little in the way of governance was actually needed in a land of dispersed family groups living in semi-isolation, at peace with each other, in mental and physical harmony with nature and the delicate teachings of the Buddha. Life had been a matter of tough existence and joyful celebration. The level of organisation required to maintain an army in this cold and vast expanse of grassland, lake and mountain would have been all but impossible. In any case, there was simply no point. Tibet had no wish to steal a country belonging to other people, no wish to cause disharmony with its neighbours, and absolutely no wish to hurt another human being in the process. Because of their inherited path of gentleness and non-violence, and their closeted view of the world, they could not understand that others would exact a most vicious holocaust on their collectively mild temperament.

News of an invasion in the east filtered through to the capital city of Lhasa in the stories of fleeing refugees. Worried whispers crossed hither and thither across the city, from monastery to hovel, across marketplaces and rivers, and there rose great consternation. They had a right to defend their culture, their land, their freedom, but their means was puny. From household to household spread the idea that they must do something to defend themselves. They were poor, unarmed and confused, but they were not cowards. From monastery to monastery, the baffled and frightened monks for the first time considered acts of self-defence which could necessarily involve violence.

Great trouble and foreboding gathered over the skies of Tibet, and the whispers of defiance gathered pace.

The clash of cultures had begun, but at first only in the head. Centuries of relative isolation had cushioned the thoughts of Tibetans from world affairs, and though the capital city had experienced occasional, and not always peaceful overtures from the British, the Moguls, the Portuguese and the Chinese before, the incidents rarely disturbed the simple pastoral existence of rural Tibetans over the long term.

Until now.

The stories of monks and nuns being paraded naked through the streets, being forced to publicly have sex with each other in town squares, under pain of death, or worse, could not be dismissed. There was horror. There was indignation, there was alarm. The burning of their precious old monasteries, their sacred texts, their exquisite wall hangings and the terrible tales of torture drove a cruel and painful wedge between the life they had led up until now, and the way they would live in the future. The Chinese army appropriated so much food that Tibetans began to starve. They were at a crossroads. A spiritual and existential crossroads.

Prayer alone was not going to solve the problem. Action was needed.

And so, on 10 March 1959, the whispers turned to words and then to actions. The peaceful Tibetans rose up to fight the mighty People's Liberation Army. Across the country, Tibetans took up their sticks and ancient muskets and fought in a vicious hand to hand combat for which they had never been trained. Thousands of women encircled the Potala Palace to shield the Dalai Lama, and Tibet became a bath of blood.

1.2 million Tibetans were slaughtered, and the Dalai Lama was forced to flee over the frozen mountains disguised as a simple farmer. Many thought him lost.

The People's Liberation Army under Mao embraced the uprising as a training exercise. From then on, the repression of Tibet was brutal and fastidious. The faceless and nameless officials moved in alongside the army to oversee the 'cleansing'. Among them were some of the vilest sadists China had ever offered.

Into this crucible of horror, Tashi was born. His fifteen years of life had never known the old Tibet, and his isolation on the high grasslands in the east of the country meant he had rarely seen a Chinese military uniform in action. His family were not the sort to seek out trouble, yet they knew the life of a modern monk was not going to be without trial.

Chapter 3
The Monastery

Labrang Monastery with its high white walls and splendidly gilded roof was as beautiful to Tashi's eyes as it was imposing. Situated high in the grasslands of Amdo, several days walk from home, it was as welcome to see as it was foreboding. The rugged mountains made an impressive backdrop. Tashi thought their snowy peaks would pierce the sky itself. The monastery was a single-storied high-ceilinged series of buildings sprawling over half a mile of uneven land. The higgledy-piggledy homes of the associated town pressed close to the monastery walls as if for comfort.

They were tired upon arrival, and his brother after having talked briefly to the older monks about this unruly sibling, stayed just one night to gather his energies for the long walk home.

They parted just as Tashi was going into the courtyard to have his first head shave. Gazing for the last time at the thick tousled locks, his brother shook his head in gentle disbelief. Tashi was not terribly good at farm work, but he would be missed in the deepest places of the heart, where true and loving affection lives. They touched foreheads and bowed. The elder brother strangely slim and lythe, the other short and stocky. Their goodbyes hinted at finality; their smiles hinted at infinity.

Tashi's new friend Jampa was younger than he and had a wicked eye for a joke and a jape. Fresh-faced and already showing signs of that dark ruddiness in the cheeks which denotes a hard life in cold climes, Jampa was the ideal companion for Tashi, though some of the older monks might have thought otherwise.

For Tashi and Jampa all life was fun. Yes, they had their studies, their wriggling meditation classes, their rituals, but there was always something to giggle at, or some crazy idea to catch hold of — like the time they started a sports club to keep everybody fit. Almost everyone joined in, even the little fat monk who was always ready to be laughed at. Tashi and Jampa invented all manner of exercises, but their favourite one was rolling over the oil drum. In this game, a large metal drum would be put on the ground and a rug placed over it. The idea was that the monks would do a sort of backwards handstand over the drum. Jampa and Tashi knew very well that many monks would not be able to do it, and the outcome was likely to be hilarious.

"Good for the back," said Jampa as he was persuading the older monks that this was a good idea.

"Very good for the arms," said Tashi, flexing his non-existent biceps with innocent eagerness.

One of the older monks weighed up the matter most carefully. "I think," said he, having noticed their sparkling eyes and impatient shuffles, "that this exercise, as you call it, is good for the spirit."

With thinly disguised elation they whooped to the courtyard where the empty drums lay waiting to be collected by the local trader. The young monks set the game up and all except the very old monks had a go. Even the more studious elders stood with kindly satisfaction to see how well the young ones were fitting in with the rhythms of monastic life. The game was a great success by any measure. Most failed the challenge with varying degrees of calamity. The fat monk fell off the drum almost as soon as he touched it, and it was so funny that inside five minutes hardly anyone could stand up for laughter. Tashi and Jampa giggled about it for days — as did practically everyone else — even though their aching muscles and bruises made it difficult. Ah, the days of guileless youth and endless laughter.

Yes, a monk's life appeared to be a good one. They understood that part of the mantle of wisdom they would eventually inherit was the sacred task of maintaining the time-honoured culture of all Tibet. The novice monks took it in their stride, only the older ones felt the weight of oppression bearing down on their slim shoulders. All around, the mountains and streams whispered stories of raids and burnings, and doors were locked at night.

The senior lamas knew it was a dangerous time to be a monk. The Chinese rule over Tibet was harsh and unforgiving. Tashi had spent his formative years of learning in some of the most distant monasteries in this, the most remote of countries. He had walked and prayed round the sacred lakes of azure blue and emerald green. He had climbed the holy mountains and wrapped his favourite shrines in colourful flags. He had walked a hundred miles of pristine grassland with little but his robes, his prayers and a wooden bowl tucked into his pocket. He had received blessings from a thousand monks and the gifts of a thousand people, for here in the most remote areas of Tibet, life had changed little. There were always the stories, of course, of the disappearances, the whispers of children losing their siblings, and the new laws, and the old laws, and nobody quite knew which were the current laws, but most of this passed Tashi by as he snuggled up by the dogs and the fire on those cold mountain evenings. This unfathomable talk was not for him.

But that unfathomable talk should have interested him. The darkness in those conversations was nothing to do with the time of day. It was the darkness entering the hearts and minds of Tibetans everywhere, for Chinese-occupied Tibet had some of the harshest restrictions on civil liberties in the world. Tashi thought he was preparing to be a monk. He did not once entertain the thought that he should be preparing for the end of his world.

The peripatetic nature of a monk's life demanded much travel, and thus, moving from monastery to monastery, Tashi and his young friend eventually found themselves in the capital city of Lhasa where the rule of law was so harshly enforced that people dare not even speak about it.

All photographs and depictions of the Dalai Lama were forbidden; to even whisper his name was forbidden. The punishment for having such a photograph, or even saying his name out loud was not clear — only that it was very bad, and thus Tashi found himself in Lhasa the day after his monastic graduation, on the Dalai Lama's birthday.

The streets and marketplaces were bursting with people, each knowing exactly what day it was, each knowing they could not say the words out loud, each celebrating with silent joy that their most revered spiritual leader was alive and well. Even though he lived away in India, exiled for life, each and every Tibetan nursed the ardent hope that one day he would return, and he would bathe them in his fathomless wisdom, and their culture of peace and beauty would be returned to them.

To an onlooker, this view of the matter may look naïve, but to a Tibetan, this was the only view. They invested their lives and hopes in a future which would bring justice and stability to their shattered culture. 1959 had been a terrible year of death and suffering, as had many years since. The mass transportation of Han Chinese into Tibet, together with the involuntary transportation of Tibetans out, was changing the demographic. The sacred lands, until then under the care of light-footed nomads, were being torn up by mining for coal and precious metals, the rivers, once so clean and bursting with life, now ran bare and dirty. The fish had given up the struggle to survive, but the hardy Tibetans had not.

It was 6 July 1988 and the bubbling excitement among the people could barely be contained. Tashi and Jampa bounced out of the monastery in high spirits, into the open spaces below the looming white walls of the Potala Palace — the place where the beloved Dalai Lama lived before his enforced exile. All around people were happily nudging against each other. Knowing glances, the clicking of tongue against cheek, merry sunburned cheeks, each sharing the joke that it was impossible for the Chinese to punish anyone for as long as they didn't actually say the forbidden words. So, choruses of 'Happy Birthday' rang out all over the massive square. At first, they were restrained, but emboldened by the lack of action from the occupying army they became louder. The small groups melded into bigger ones until the entire city was jostling and jumping and shouting 'Happy birthday!'.

Whether it was the misplaced sense of liberation, even the ability to shout something, anything, at the top of their voices, or the communal sense of being uplifted, or if it was simply the fact that it was the Dalai Lama's birthday and the heavens shone so brightly on the glistening walls of the Potala Palace it is hard to say, but someone in the crowd became fatally emboldened.

"Happy birthday, Dalai Lama!" came the lone voice.

The crowd stopped chanting. The Chinese soldiers, who themselves had almost seemed to be enjoying the occasion, stood straight. Then someone else shouted, "Happy birthday, Dalai Lama!", and the mould was set.

A man pulled a crumpled photograph out of his pocket and held it high. "Happy birthday, Dalai Lama!"

Another man did the same. Then a woman. Then a monk.

The crowd stirred visibly. In a matter of minutes, the mood went from boisterous fun to outright defiance. Everything had changed. Years of oppressive rule, of disappearances, of joblessness, of cultural suffocation and cruelty, had turned this naturally docile and forgiving people into, just for one moment, a crowd of anger and defiance.

Tashi and Jampa were quickly wrapped up in the mood as everyone started congratulating themselves on this spontaneous act of rebellion, and they started jumping about madly and shouting the forbidden words at the top of their voices. Tashi had a mangled photograph of the young Dalai Lama hidden deep in his pocket. He tore it out and held it as high as he could. It was jubilation, it was freedom, it was release. Who could stop so many people singing the words in one happy voice?

Then gunshots.

The Chinese state of mind and the Tibetan state of mind could not have been further apart.

Soldiers lined up at the front of the crowd, visors down, bayonets fixed, guns pointing. They shot into the crowd again. Live rounds of course. This time it registered. But it was confusing. Those near the site of the shootings tried to drag the fallen away, those at the back continued to shout the forbidden words. In every mind were three questions: What was there to gain? What was there to lose? Where to run?

The world outside Tibet evidenced little support and turned its ubiquitous blind eye. China in 1988 was becoming a significant trading partner for many developed countries. To the rest of the world, there was money to be made in keeping quiet. China was a low wage economy, it had practically no environmental laws, and the waste and pollution from manufacturing goods for other countries was uncounted in the calculation of cost. Everyone was buying cheap from China and they wanted to keep it that way. Who cared that the rivers, the seas and the air would be polluted to the point of irreversibility, just as long as the rivers of New York ran clean, and the skies over London were breathable, no one was going to mess with China? There was nothing to gain from supporting the hapless Tibetans, and a lot of cheap consumer goods to lose. The rule of the neo-liberal was the only rule. Profit and consumption at any cost was the international game of the day.

Could Tibetans win back their country in this heartfelt but insignificant moment of insurrection? They knew they could not. And so, the shouting became more hesitant, the photographs were hastily stuffed back into pockets, and the moment of bravado blew away in the diminishing spring breeze.

Jampa tugged at the robes of his friend who was still holding the forbidden image in his hand. "Put it away, quickly, or they will see you."

But Tashi was still a bit carried away with happiness. He hadn't been as perceptive as his friend, or maybe he just processed the information a little more slowly. In any case, the square was emptying fast and the place to be was anywhere but there.

Jampa quailed inside as his quick eyes noticed that they had been spotted. "Come quickly, Tashi. Tashi, quickly."

He dragged his friend as fast as he could. Tashi seemed to be labouring under the peculiar impression that he was immune to arrest, or maybe invisible to the Chinese, and did not seem to rush.

Jampa saw it coming, Tashi did not. The blow to the back of his head knocked him unconscious, and Jampa did not leave him. They dragged Tashi away, the photograph of the Dalai Lama fluttering forlornly to the ground.

Sweet-natured Jampa begged them to let Tashi go. In return, he was kicked in the face. Beautiful white teeth crushed, face running with blood.

Poor Jampa. He would be dead within the year. Head crushed under the brown boot of a Chinese sadist.

Chapter 4
Firenza

She bought the ticket with mixed feelings. They were all allowed one flight a year before the carbon taxes made flying impossibly expensive. It had been an impulse. As if to get to the root of one problem she felt it necessary to get to the root of something else. Her two-week holiday window had arrived, and she needed to do something different, go somewhere different, escape the baffling culture of wanting everything and needing little. She needed a tonic for the soul, and thus, in one of her more extravagant crescendos of thought, she decided on Tibet.

Quite what she would do when she got there was another matter, but that was of little concern to a young woman to whom opportunity regularly presented itself, and for which she was usually readily available. There was enough of a palaver sorting out the flat she had shared until recently with her boyfriend Tom. In fairness, he wasn't exactly her boyfriend, though at one time she thought he might be. At one time he probably thought he was, but that was a while back. The flat was too small to hold anything much, and they were too broke to have anything much. They sorted through the few bizarre things they had collected. The colourful but broken Chinese temple dog; three matching soup bowls of somewhat Japanese origin; some plates which did not match but with which Firenza felt an affinity; a frameless poster on the wall of birch trees in winter, pinned at the corners, looking resilient in the winter's snow; various bits of bedding; a crazy light fitting made of coloured plastic; some pots and pans... What was hers, what was his? It took a few minutes — it was mostly hers.

Theirs had been a flat-sharing of convenience more than anything. They liked each other well enough, but the task of affording a place to live in an expensive city was daunting. There was only one bedroom, and only one bed. There was a sitting room with a cupboard of a kitchen over which the stairs climbed, and a bathroom at the top. Tom gave up the uncomfortable sofa at her behest with a curious mixture of guilt and promised comfort. Guilt that he was paying less than half of her mortgage costs, even though he slept on the couch, jostling with the ever-present need for human comfort, touch, and companionship. They lived like an old married couple. They occasionally had sex, which was OK, but it didn't exactly make the earth move, they had little arguments about toothpaste, or who was doing the shopping next, and they shared the chores. It might have been economically satisfying, but it was not emotionally satisfying. He found a less convenient, but more loving girlfriend, and inevitably moved out.

Firenza liked her. No tears, no tribulations, but there was the mortgage to pay. Firenza resolved to think about that after her little holiday.

Planning the journey would keep her occupied — and then there was work. Always a hard and diligent worker, her colleagues were at pains to point out that managing without her would be impossible. They were being kind. She loved to take on new clients but tidying up the loose ends was always time-consuming.

Firenza was an arts graduate with a hearty dislike for anything commercial. Perversely she had a job in advertising. It was ludicrous how she fell into such a job, but she was creative and it was a lucrative outlet for her talents. More than once, she questioned what she was doing, and who she was doing it for. More than once, she thought she should quit. But options were slim and the mortgage for her small flat in the centre of London had trapped her in the rat race, the rat trap, the poverty trap. Onwards and upwards she would say to herself, but she never quite knew where she was going.

"Tibet," she announced to enquiring colleagues.

A dozen pairs of eyebrows went into moderate orbit.

"It'll make a change," and she slapped down her laptop with irrepressible finality, grinned broadly, strode briskly out the door, skirt swaying, scarf trailing, bag hitting the doorframe on her way out, as always.

Friends would laugh that she left a trail of devastation in her wake wherever she went. But it was far from the truth. She was thoughtful and kind, tinged with the kind of wackiness which bordered on, but never quite identified itself as, eccentric. The kind of clothes she wore bore out her sense of individuality. She wore hats when no one wore hats. She wore workmen's boots one day and precarious stiletto heels the next. She could be a style icon taken straight out of the pages of a 1950s' *Vogue* magazine, or a post-punk leftover. How she would appear from one day to the next was, shall we say, unpredictable, and the beauty of it all was that she was largely unaware of how she looked. It was a constant source of entertainment to all who thought they knew her.

What was not up for debate was her urgent honesty and her default kindness. She took time to talk to the homeless man on the corner of her building, often bringing him coffee and biscuits, sometimes money. Her tiny flat was always littered with the detritus of other people staying over for a day, or a week, or more. It didn't bother her that there was barely enough space for one. If someone needed a place to stay, she was first to offer. Maybe they would help her out with food and expenses; maybe they wouldn't. Firenza definitely did not belong in advertising, but advertising wanted her to stay and paid enough to keep her.

There was only one quick way to get to Tibet and that was via Kathmandu airport in Nepal. She would love to have taken a train all the way, but two weeks' holiday would barely have left her enough time to get there one way and certainly not enough for a return journey. As it was, the arrangements were complicated enough. It troubled her that she would need Chinese permission to enter Tibet and it slowly began to enter her consciousness that Tibet was not the independent and spiritual country at the top of the world she had envisaged it to be. Her hurried information gathering of Tibetan history and politics was rather too hurried. She was young and still harboured romantic notions of peaceful meditations in warm monasteries surrounded by breathtaking scenery.

She was right about the scenery though. As they left Kathmandu airport bound for Lhasa, the small aircraft skimmed the lower mountains and she drew in her breath. The rivers below snaked and divided like a nest of cobras. And brown, it was all a million shades of silver granite and tawny brown. Patches of snow here and there denoted the very high peaks. At lower altitudes, a few little fields farmed into neat stripes looked like impossibly pathetic attempts to stamp the mark of humanity on the landscape, for the towering bleakness of sharp granite crowned all and left an indelible mark on Firenza's mind. It was going to be a very different holiday.

She had booked a package holiday with a holiday company just for convenience — not that there was a lot of choice in the matter. Her plan was to use the hotel as a base, but sneak off with her rucksack and explore for herself this land of legend. It was not the plan the Chinese authorities had in mind.

The group she found herself conjoined with was mostly made up of middle-aged couples, several being Buddhist practitioners, whose call to this place was purely spiritual. Admittedly she did not actually understand what they were talking about as they mutually pondered the different types of Buddhism, yogic practices and thangkas, but she nodded in some of the right places. There were some would-be Buddhists and a scattering of people who looked as if they might have some business or purpose in these parts. Oddly, there were no actual Tibetans, which was disappointing as she would have liked to have some first-hand knowledge of the situation before embarking on her small expeditions. She had yet to experience the crucifying poverty of the majority of Tibetan people.

The tour guide greeted them at the airport ceremoniously with a grinning "Tashi Delek" and placed a white scarf, the khata, round each of their necks, bowing profusely and wishing them a happy stay, long life and a few other things it was difficult to understand. They took it all in the spirit in which it was intended, some bowing with hands clasped, others looking a bit bewildered, bowing uncomfortably, and wondering what to do with their hands, or their eyes, or their bodies. Firenza was in the latter category. She had never bowed with clasped hands, but she always knew how to smile and did so to great effect as she stooped to let the smaller tour guide reach over her head. He grinned back. It felt like a primitive rapport.

The Himalayan Yak Hotel was situated on one of the main streets close to the Potala Palace, with a colourfully painted traditional reception room of red, with bursts of blue and green, and white swirls of fantastical beasts. Firenza wanted to study the patterns and discover their origins and meanings. The designs were unlike anything in the West and appealed to her creative instincts. The colours were in blocks. The stylised flowers and trees, neither Chinese nor Indian, but with hints of a far orient of distant times, were neatly sorted and filed in the graphic department of her brain for future reference.

The sweetly smiling staff ushered them through the small hotel lobby. It had a gentle air of tranquillity about it — possibly enhanced by the lack of background music which seemed to accompany practically every space in the western world. Firenza's room was simple, neatly arranged and comfortable. The highly polished wooden floors and handwoven rugs allowed an aura of cleanliness, but also a significant cultural difference, for woven rugs made by hand barely existed in the UK. The bedside lamps were hand-carved with printed paper shades, and the bedcover was again a hand-spun wonder of applique and tiny stitches. She loved it all. Life in the so-called West had relinquished the very idea of cottage industries in favour of mass production, container loads of imports and man-made fibres. The great irony being that whilst the poorer sections of eastern Asia were manufacturing cheap mass-produced goods for Western consumption, they were themselves committed to the cultural values of their own identity. She would like one of those bedcovers, she thought. They felt more real than something made by machine — more honest.

The first night she slept surprisingly well on the hard bed and elected to have breakfast outside on the roof terrace. The sun was barely up and it was crispy cold outside, but the mountain air was still and she relished the thought of breathing the thin air deeply. At this height of nearly four thousand metres, she was indeed breathing more deeply and, to her, this was a fine thing. Crystal clean air. Far, far from the polluted streets of London. It was a privilege she wanted to become addicted to.

Bananas, porridge and honey seemed to be the right thing to eat, so she found the spot where the sun shed its first morning light and, muffled and wrapped in her layers of fleece, she ate the best breakfast of her life.

A small backpack was ready by her side, so after she had eaten, she threw it across her shoulder, strode past reception and out into the street to greet her first full day in Lhasa.

Hurried footsteps followed her. "Please, miss. Your itinerary. Very nice time. You wait with others." The speaker looked to be little more than a girl in age, bowing profusely as she spoke, pleading, trying to guide Firenza back into the hotel.

"Please, miss. You wait for group. Very nice here. You sit for a while."

Firenza had no intention of sitting anywhere, nor did she want to wait for a group of any sort. She wanted to get on with an adventure, and the very first part of that was to explore her immediate surroundings.

"It's OK," she said calmly. "I'm just going out for a look around."

Shadows of panic passed the young girl's face. Clearly, Firenza had not actually read the small print: 'lots to see, knowledgeable guides, plenty of arranged trips. The fine detail was there by omission. 'Plenty of arranged trips' said it all. There was only group travel.

The immense grandeur of Tibet, its lakes, its mountains, its monasteries, its people, its towns and villages were all off limits — unless, of course, you had a registered tour guide, in which case everything outside the prescribed visitor schedule would be off limits.

Had Firenza planned her trip more carefully, or maybe read the information she was given more judiciously, she would have realised that there was very little free time, lots of planned excursions and a great deal of waiting around, but she had booked this holiday in a hurry and used the intervening few days to plan what she would like to do and not what the Chinese government would like her to do.

She allowed herself to be led back into the hotel. "Is for you safety, you see?" said the beaming young girl, as she poured tea from a shining samovar, offering it with gentle poise, a deep bow and no eye contact.

Firenza was bemused, but compliant, for the time being. She accepted the small cup of liquid and tried to get an internet signal on her smartphone. She didn't think she had signed up for anything in the way of group excursions, so needed to check everything more carefully.

A kerfuffle of voices and movement distracted her efforts. It was the rest of the group she had travelled with coming down to the foyer. She recognised some of them from the airport in Kathmandu. The woman with brown wiry hair was chatting animatedly to the man with straight brown hair, who nodded sagely as he guided his nervous-looking wife along as if she was a flighty poodle. She, in fact, looked very much like a flighty poodle with her hair too yellow and frizzly, all plumped up on top, begging for a little red bow to complete the similarity. Where Firenza was dressed in walking boots, fisherman's trousers, a shirt and two fleece jackets — one across her shoulders, one tied loosely round her waist — the poodle lady was wearing a pair of white linen trousers, slingback sandals and a frilly blouse. A cream jacket hung over her arm. She looked as if she was going on an expedition to deepest suburbia for a calorie-controlled lunch. Not that Firenza was entirely sensible with her own dress, for she sported huge Cuban earrings, which rattled slightly when she shook her head, and an outrageously colourful scarf depicting tigers and leopards and bright green jungle leaves. Firenza was the sort of person who could not melt into the background if she tried.

Having virtually no prior knowledge of the political situation in Tibet, Firenza judged it best to play along with whatever the tour operator had laid out, at least for the first day. She had very little travel experience and had paid scant attention to current affairs unless they affected her job or people she knew, so, in a position of near-perfect ignorance, she was neither particularly compliant nor in the mood for revolt. It was a fresh mountain day after all and she just wanted to hurry out and enjoy it.

But wait she must. The woman with the brown wiry hair looked as though travelling ran through her veins. Every thread of her attire seeped practicality, from her multi-pocketed, multi-zipped khaki trousers, to her multi-layered selection of shirt, waistcoat, weatherproof jacket, and hat. The hat even had a pocket on one side. Firenza stifled a smile as the Mad Hatter came to mind, for there was enough room for a small white ticket proclaiming ten shillings and six pence. Lewis Carroll would have been impressed. The rucksack on the woman's back was light and far from full, but in it was a tool for every emergency — or so Firenza imagined.

She introduced herself as Margot and sat down beside Firenza, deftly shifting the position of the rucksack to one side as she leaned back against the red velvet chair.

"It's not likely that we will get much time on our own," she offered in the kind of voice which could cower an invading army. An understanding smile spreading warmly across her face. "They won't want any 'incidents'." The last word was said in conspiratorial parenthesis. It felt as though an elbow nudge was imminent.

Firenza caught sight of the battered leather walking boots on the other woman's feet. Margot looked like a reliable source of information.

"Such a lovely day," sighed Firenza, and introduced herself. "Some call me Fira, but Firenza is good too."

"Hi. I guess you haven't been to Tibet before. Have you done much travelling?" Margot's voice assumed the timbre of a schoolteacher questioning a group of unruly boys in the playground.

Firenza thought about that. How to decide what was travelling and what was a holiday. There seemed to be a world of difference, judging by Margot's boots. In fact, if footwear was the judge of anything, the poodle lady in her slingbacks was going to have trouble getting out of a taxi, Margot was about to launch a single-handed assault on K2, and well, Firenza was somewhere in-between. Maybe she had put herself into the position of having an adventurous holiday. More correctly she had booked a holiday, which looked interesting enough to be considered an adventure. Her new walking boots reflected more the certain knowledge that they were surrounded by mountains than the aptitude of their owner as a traveller by nature. Firenza's shiny boots could not compare with the worn, scuffed, slightly dusty, and still eminently serviceable footwear peeking out from under Margot's frighteningly practical trousers. For a moment Firenza imagined a compass, a map, a piece of string and a sixpenny bit hiding in those pockets. That was it. Margot looked like the Girl Guide leader she had experienced way back when she was about ten years old, and under whose influence she had learned how to tie reef knots behind her back, light fires and sew various badges of girlish achievement onto the sleeve of her blue Girl Guides' blouse. She had thought that Guiding would be an adolescent rite of passage of some sort. Instead, she had found it all rather tedious. Firenza had been a Girl Guide for almost two months and her leader had given the impression of being worthy, but not worldly. Margo, at roughly twice her age, at least promised to be more worldly.

"Booking this was a bit of a rush job," said Firenza in reply. "I don't really have any expectations other than to learn something of this unusual land and its customs."

"Well, be careful," said Margot as discretely as she could, given her natural level of decisive decibels. "This is Occupied Land."

Firenza's head was assaulted by more than one question, but they came out on one word. "Occupied?"

"Yes. The Chinese have taken full control and the Tibetans don't like it. You see, they are largely prevented from taking part in the customs and rituals of their culture. Even their language is under threat. I have heard that a Tibetan cannot get a job unless he or she speaks Chinese. That's roughly why I am here — to find out for myself how it is. Not that I will be allowed to discover much. They keep a careful eye on us." And she nodded discreetly in the direction of a uniformed guard at the hotel entrance who Firenza had not previously noticed.

Margot continued, in slightly hushed tones, which was almost an impossibility. "I'm a curious sort of person. The Chinese government wouldn't want any trouble with tourists, so I might just push my luck here and there."

It's fair to say that Firenza was a bright enough person, if a little unworldly, and known to be quick on the uptake. "Right. I see." She scanned the hotel foyer where visitors were milling around. "I'm getting it, a bit. So, are you a journalist?"

Margot laughed quietly. She was not going to admit to anything. "Ah, I see our group is about to receive some instruction. Let's go over."

They learned about their itinerary from the allocated guide, a slight and bowing man, with greased back hair which looked as though every strand had been picked up and parked in the wrong direction. There appeared to be an ongoing struggle between the stylist and mother nature, whereby the stylist wanted it slicked back into a neat head-hugging shape and nature wanted it to stand up on end, vertical, as if he was in a permanent state of horripilation. Of this battle, he was abundantly aware, and he rubbed his hands across his head with feverish regularity in order to keep the unresting mane, tamed. Genetics would doom him to everlasting failure.

The guide introduced himself as Wen Wangdu and, with an overwhelming selection of bows and smiles, told them where they would be going each day, what time they would be leaving, and hidden between the lines were little clues as to what would be expected from them, the visitors. It was all very charming and polite. And prescriptive. And claustrophobic.

Firenza picked up the instruction that they were not to lose sight of their guide, all excursions had to be properly permitted, and the safest way to see as much of Tibet as could be possible in two weeks was to go on the excursions planned by his good self under the experienced management of the renowned tour operator. He omitted to say it was the only way.

It seemed reasonable to do as she was told, so Firenza chatted to the dozen or so other people on her trip to gather their thoughts on the matter. Most of them were content to be bundled around from hotel to coach and back again, so it seemed the most interesting choice of companion was likely to be Margot.

From Margot she heard that Tibet, but especially Lhasa, was crammed with secret police, uniformed army and millions of Han Chinese brought overland to

Tibet with financial inducements to settle the land and therefore dilute the population of native Tibetans. In the opposite direction, Tibetans were being taken to China for 'education'. No one knows how many. No one speaks of it. All were afraid of it.

Over those first few days of sightseeing and monasteries and windswept mountain scenery, Firenza developed an entirely different outlook on life. She was careful not to appear as naïve as she actually was and Margot was careful not to have these discussions in places where they could be overheard.

Slowly the so-called holiday became a voyage of enlightenment — but not in the way Firenza had imagined. She thought she would be steeped in Tibetan Buddhist culture, instead, she was forced to see Tibet, and indeed the world, in an entirely different way. Politically, her eyes were opening.

Where once Firenza had believed the news, now she was peering round the edges of what was reported. Where once she had thought her country was good and honest, she was discovering that it was neither. It was bewildering at first, but Firenza had an open mind and was mature enough to entertain thoughts contrary to her current beliefs.

She did not know that a full-scale assault on her guileless understanding was just a few hours away.

They were on an obligatory coach tour. The day was clear, the air was pristine. The coach driver was almost terrifying in casual competence as they wound around the snaking Himalayan roads. It was an unsettling way to start the day, watching the coach repeatedly aiming perilously close to the edge of a sickening drop, the front of the vehicle overhanging, then violently turning away from the very jaws of death in the kind of lurch which could leave no stomach, unchurned. After repeating this a hundred times, the stomach still lurched, but the panic settled into a sense of fatalism. Maintaining a constant state of terror was not sustainable. 'If we go over, we go over', was probably what everybody eventually thought. Even the poodle lady had given up digging her lacquered nails into her husband's arm every time a corner appeared — which was about every three minutes. The lessons of the mountains were easy. This was no place for wheeled transport. This was a place of snow leopards, yaks and soaring birds. The stoic humans who eked out a life in this strange and beautiful land did so at their peril and they understood their place on this vast plateau of life.

The monastery on this day's itinerary was Drepung. One of the biggest in Tibet. It nestled comfortably into the side of a mountain with its pretty tiled roofs and whitewashed walls. A barely significant human touch amongst the uncompromising awe of Himalayan grandeur. It was much bigger than Firenza expected.

A maroon clad monk was slowly sweeping the steps that lead to a small stupa. A group of Tibetans, gathered inside, spinning prayer wheels of shiny brass markings. Buddhists would, daily, if not more often, visit these monastery wheels and spin the gleaming drums with their hands in the hope of accumulating merit and wisdom and purifying negativity. Often, they would softly chant mantras as the wheels spun, the transformative 'Om mani padme hum' being the time-honoured favourite. In spinning the wheels, the Buddhists would hope to multiply their good karma a million-fold. It was a useful technology, thought Firenza, enabling a swifter path to enlightenment in a shorter time. She smiled to herself, imagining the prayer wheels as the pocket calculators of the karmic world.

The monastery looked like a place for quiet social gatherings as well as prayer, or maybe it was simply a place to preserve the Tibetan way of life. Unhurried, unthreatening, unmarred by thoughts of profit and the rat race, humans blending with nature in the morning mist which hung around the golden roofs of the holy building. Two monks draped in traditional robes of maroon and saffron, one arm bare, the other covered in folded cloth, emerged from their morning devotions, heads together as if discussing something of high importance. The robes themselves were probably the oldest form of dress still in use, dating from 2,500 years ago. They were versatile, their patchwork construction was easily repairable, they were simple and they were honest. It was all a million miles away from Firenza's home, where fashion ruled the streets of London. Often impractical, often expensive and too often treated as disposable, she could feel the distance between this culture and her own widening into an impassable gulf. To her, the robes signified something lost. The structures of spirituality in the Western world had been torn down and replaced with consumerism and celebrity and fast food. She wondered just how compromised her way of life could be, removed from nature as it inevitably was, dirty and polluting, inconsiderate and brutal. She began to assess just how much she could learn from these people.

"Most of it was destroyed back in the fifties," whispered Margot as the coach parked on a convenient precipice. "There used to be six thousand monks here, now apparently only three hundred are allowed."

Firenza stared. The place was vast. More a university than a monastery. A place where monks and nuns would study the working of the inner mind for twelve hours a day. Where science and languages were taught, where study and analysis of the six major religions was compulsory. A place of meditation and deep thought, spirituality and order. Except that it wasn't.

"Why?" she asked Margot simply, almost distractedly, as she gazed upon the soaring white walls of Drepung with their hundreds of windows topped by red and gold roofs.

"Religion is the sign of the oppressed creature, the heart of a heartless world, and the soul of soulless conditions. It is the opium of the people. Mao. I wrote it down. Look." And she tilted her notebook towards Firenza.

"I remember that last bit, but the rest is new to me. Heart of a heartless world. Interesting. You'd think a heartless world would need a heart more than anything."

"Not according to Mao. 'Purging' was his middle name. He wasn't too keen on sparrows either."

"Sparrows?"

"Yup. Under Mao, birds were declared to be the public animals of capitalism.

"Why on earth pick on the sparrows?" retorted Firenza, concerned and bemused at the same time.

"They ate the grain which was meant for people. A task force of about three million people was sent out to kill them."

Firenza thought about the little house sparrows which were a common feature of British gardens. Small, not especially colourful, with their brownish looks and intelligent little eyes. How weird was the legendary Chairman Mao if he had to wage a war on sparrows?

Margot continued, happy to tell someone these quirky details of history. "The Chinese would bang pots and pans all day and all night. The sparrows could not perch and rest with the noise all around. After two days they just fell out of the sky, stone dead."

Firenza shook her head. "Poor sparrows. That is so cruel."

"Indeed. They were pushed to the brink of extinction. Hundreds of millions of sparrows were killed in this way. It was ridiculously self-defeating too, because anyone with a whiff of knowledge would know that the sparrows ate many of the pests which would destroy the rice crops. The locust population increased massively; the rice harvest dwindled. Total incompetence if you ask me. If you tamper with ecology in ignorance of the effect it may have, you court disaster. The Great Leap Forward became a murderous fall backwards with all the madcap experiments with pesticides and poisons. Ecological mismanagement was a primary cause of the famine which killed forty million people."

Firenza had next to no knowledge about recent Chinese history, and if she had thought she was going to China she would have at least done a bit of reading on the subject. As it was, she thought she was going to Tibet, except that Tibet was not actually the top-of-the-world ancient culture her loosely gathered information, or maybe her active imagination, had envisaged. Her views on this part of the world were in flux as thoughts of ancient spirituality tussled with the new concepts Margot had put forward. It was an uneasy mix, and a strange sense of foreboding began to form a cloud in her bright and enquiring mind.

Firenza was a quiet atheist. When you simply do not believe in a divine being, all-seeing, all-knowing, there is nothing to shout about. She had always toyed with mystical belief systems, curiosity being her nature, but she had never believed in any god, and because nothing could be proved either way in terms of his or her existence, no one could persuade her that there was anything other than the world as it was, and she was developing a growing concern that this world was not being properly looked after by those who purported to have its best interests at heart. She didn't think about politics too much, because she was young, unworldly and gifted with the kind of joy for life which left the unprepared exhausted. If you asked her what she believed in, she might say 'nothing much', because there was little point to her in believing in anything material, or human, or even an imagined supernatural being. It was a matter of trust. She adored nature and the elements — especially extremes like storms and lightning and sudden snow falling many feet deep, but she didn't 'believe' in them. It was clear that they existed, but it was a mad idea to confer an unequivocal religious conviction upon worldly elements, even if they disguised themselves as liquid, solid or, at times, gas. Science was interesting, not magical.

In any case, blind deference was not in her DNA. It was a simple fact. Like being vegan. No one could persuade her that cruelty in animal slaughter was not present, so the matter was not up for debate and she minimised her culpability in the cruelty by not eating animal products. She sometimes ruminated on thoughts that if there had been some sort of divine being with goodness as a goal, the world might have turned out better. As it was, the diverse mixture of humanity crawling across the planet embraced little in the way of real goodness. That was something she hoped to find out more about up here on the roof of the world, but nothing is as it seems, and her previous goal of understanding Buddhism was inevitably changing to having to understand the ways of the Chinese government.

The coach was not full. The little clutch of people from the Himalayan Yak Hotel obediently disembarked and wound their way towards the monastery in bedraggled fashion, jackets dripping from hastily gathered bags, hats slightly askew and muted conversation between them as befits entrance to a holy place.

The monastery at Drepung was all but deserted. A few armed Chinese guards stood around trying to look casual and failing. No one in army uniform brandishing a gun and bayonet, in public, could look anything but menacing. Firenza didn't like it. She wasn't used to it. The police in the UK did not brandish guns and the army was not on the streets. Any gun held by anybody was to her a death threat and she kept a wily distance.

Margot nudged Firenza's arm and her eyes pointed up to a camera in the eaves of the building. It was well hidden and it briefly crossed Firenza's mind that it was strange, amongst the glorious artwork of the temple entrance, that Margot would even be noticing a tiny camera.

As they walked through the overhanging porch towards one of the more beautifully decorated entrance doors, Margot subtly pointed out other surveillance cameras. They were well hidden, but obviously not well enough for Margot's prying eyes.

Exotically painted doors of red and green and white and azure greeted them. The stylised patterns of flowers in full bloom were picked out in shimmering gold. Polished brass hinges surrounded by carvings of shapes she could not fathom, and pictures of some she could, opened gently in front of them, and inside... Firenza gasped. The walls were covered in priceless silk hangings from floor to ceiling. Each one composed of millions of intricate stitches and worked with a thousand bright colours. It was more than breathtaking. Yet, partially hidden amongst these fabulously ancient thangkas, it was possible to see more cameras. It was unsettling.

Firenza set off to look around the large prayer hall. She automatically went to the right. And was immediately corrected. They had to go clockwise — not that she could see it mattered. Hardly anyone was there. Maybe it was bad luck to go the wrong way round.

The woman with the yellow hair had abandoned her slingbacks in favour of gold plastic trainers. It was like watching the clash of civilisations replay time and again as she tried to ask a lone monk something he did not understand. He bowed most courteously; she spoke a little louder. He looked helpless; she tried again, this time with hand gestures, clattering her wrists covered with gold coloured bling, and the monk understood even less. He bowed and smiled broadly. It was a little pantomime that may never have been resolved had the tour guide not intervened.

Out of the corner of her eye, Firenza could see one of the long red drapes dividing the main hall from other parts of the temple twitching. It was on the opposite side of the room. Margot saw it at the same time and moved quietly in that direction.

The little pantomime with the yellow-haired woman had gathered a few tourists. Firenza could not catch what they were saying, but the yellow-haired lady was being insistent about something which no one present appeared to have an answer to. Something about a goddess, or a Tara which should have been somewhere or other and was not. It was fairly hard to believe that this frizzy blond knew any details about these places at all, but Firenza did not judge. Life was full of nothing if not surprises.

The curtain in the corner was twitching in a more agitated fashion. Margot, who had wandered off in an air of magnificent nonchalance, ostensibly to do her own thing, was right there, the curtain drew back just a bit and behind it were three faces. Not the usual smiling faces of open-hearted Tibetans, but three frightened, agitated faces, beckoning frantically to Margot.

It was much too interesting for Firenza to ignore and much more interesting than the floor show across the room, so she sidled quietly down one of the aisles to join Margot.

She saw a piece of paper pushed into Margot's hand. Margot pushed it to Firenza quickly, who, grasping that this might be important, and in any case was subterfuge of some form or another, shoved it into her pocket and tried to affect a look of blithe unconcern. Then the worried faces of the monks turned to panic and a uniformed man wearing shiny brown boots appeared from behind them. Scuffling and muffled cries could be heard, then the curtain became still, and the horrified Wen Wandgu rushed up to retrieve his errant tourists, all bows and smiles.

"Please, you stay with me," insisted the guide. "We have nice time, but all together. Understand?"

They nodded, smiling back amiably, wondering what had just happened.

The guide, twitching visibly, ushered them back outside into the fresh mountain air, clucking like a mother hen. "We walk this way," he gestured encouragingly. "Come. Come now. Now."

Whilst the group was pulling itself together outside the main temple, a grey uniformed man stepped out to stop them. He wanted to ask Margot some questions.

"Just for one minute." He tried to smile, but it looked dishonest. His voice was soft, but with guttural undertones. Firenza took an immediate dislike to him and his shiny brown boots. His expression appeared to be in direct contradiction to his thoughts.

He led Margot to one side and started questioning her. His back was towards Firenza, shielding most of Margot's slight figure.

Firenza stayed obediently with the group and opened a conversation with the man with straight hair who sported a persistently worried look. She did not check her pocket, she tried to look interested in some architecture nearby, asking if he knew the age of that building, knowing cameras were everywhere, wondering what was on that folded piece of paper, or maybe in it.

She had to bottle her curiosity, even though her mind became unrealistically convinced that the little screwed up note in her pocket had expanded into a huge wad of secrets bulging out of her trousers for all to see.

The air seemed to hum with anticipation. There was a tinge of fear about the place. Indefinable, but Firenza could sense a new mood, a heavy stillness you could cut with a knife. Torn between the need to look casual and the need to see what was happening behind her, she tried not to show concern as Margot was led away.

Their guide was hiding his increasing state of apoplexy with difficulty. His carefully slicked back hair was planning to revolt. One patch was showing distinct signs of disobedience and had broken free of the oily slick and was standing upright. He sensed the drama on his scalp and drew his hand backwards over his head to quell the gathering protest.

"We go to next temple," he said. "Come. Come now. Now." He forced a smile. It was not the usual guileless Tibetan smile, it was a timid smile, hiding fright, hiding inner sweat.

Firenza was torn between behaving as though nothing was wrong, expressing concern over Margot, or causing a downright fuss about the situation.

"I think we should wait for Margot," she eventually said. The yellow-haired woman surprisingly agreed and others nodded. Solidarity didn't seem to be a word evident in any of the bystanders' usual vocabulary, but it was heartening that they felt they should stand by one of their number.

Their guide looked even more troubled if that was possible. He wanted less than nothing to do with the Chinese security forces. He weighed up the odds of demotion, or worse if there was an argument in the monastery streets about it. With a sinking head, he weighed the conundrum heavily. He had a wife and children, an elderly mother, and a disabled cousin to look after. They all depended on his small salary.

His shoulders shrunk, visibly. He would go and enquire. The troublesome patch of hair now pointing to the sky.

Chapter 5
The Monk. Nine Years Later

The great authoritarian regimes, not knowing what to do with their psychopaths, their sociopaths and their sadists, gave them a uniform, promoted them, and sent them off to the far reaches of the Empire. Here they could do their worst, unimpeded by oversight, decency or behavioural norms. Here they tortured, maimed and raped — the innocent as much as the guilty. Here they could feed their insatiable appetites with all the cruelty and bloodlust they could get. In return, there was only the monthly report back to a distant capital, unimpressed and uncaring. Such reports were always on a need-to-know basis. The only reports the authorities were interested in reading were the ones that told them the natives were quiet and all was under control. The authorities always got the reports they wanted.

Li Enlai both took pride in what he did and was simultaneously disgusted by it. He looked at the broken body on the floor and, for a moment, felt compassion, then was offended, as if the job was not good enough or had not met expectations. His lip curled in disdainful arrogance. He spat.

The tortured remains were thrown out onto the street.

Kind arms picked up the lifeless form under cover of darkness. They half carried, half dragged the body to an ancient house, the entrance of which was teetering on the brink of collapse, in a dark and dingy alleyway, far from the bustle of busy streets.

In silence, they laid him gently on the floor. His body broken, his face lumpy, cracked and bleeding, an eye hanging out of its socket, the skull deformed from vicious blows. They folded the remains of his red robes around him, tucking them across his body as if he was a child at bedtime.

They did not know his name, only that he was a monk, yet another monk thrown out of the darkness of the nearby prison, at night, presumed dead. If he had been their brother, he would be unrecognisable to them, but in a sense, he was their brother. He was a Tibetan, a Buddhist, a monk. Their duty to him was the same as their duty to each other — to offer love and compassion, support and sustenance, wherever it was needed.

Cross-legged, the two men sat on the stone floor beside the body, offering their prayers and tears. They had seen this type of cruelty so many times before, yet it seemed always to be the first time, such was the shock of the injuries before them. But this monk was not yet cold, his skin retained elasticity, and it was barely discernible, but the fingers on one hand seemed to twitch, so faintly, that the mourners thought they might have blinked, but they interrupted their prayers to check.

The taller one put his head to the monk's chest and felt his wrist for a pulse. Yes, it was there, something was there. It was impossible, but there was life.

These two kindly men had once been monks. Monastic life had not been ideal for them, though they tried to make it fit. The taller one had been hyperactive as a child. Always in trouble with the older lamas, unable to sit still enough for meditation and prone to a secret habit of smoking (which was, in fact, no secret at all — for who could mistake the smell of a cigarette on a monk's breath), he nonetheless was devoted to his monastery and, when he reached his seventeenth birthday, all agreed that he would make a very suitable driver to take visiting monks and dignitaries around the country. It was a happy compromise.

But now the Chinese had invaded he was no longer needed. The capital of Tibet had, to all intents and purposes, de-camped to North India. The monasteries had been forcibly disbanded, with only a tiny fraction of monks allowed to stay, and travel was not allowed. Virtual prisoners in their own culture, their own country, they were the last bastions of the old Tibetan life. Dissent was met with swift and irrevocable punishment. The remaining monks bowed their heads in sadness and shrank from the public eye.

The shorter man had also been a monk and had enjoyed the life and the opportunities for learning it offered, and yet it did not offer him quite enough. He had met a woman and wanted to marry, to have a family and pursue more varied interests. It was quite possible to be a monk and to be married, but he had chosen to move in more worldly circles. Always devoted to his calling as a Buddhist, he had found himself living near Drapchi prison and could not turn away from the broken bodies thrown out at night. It was a job that needed doing. There was no pay as such, but his countrywomen and men looked after his wife and children with food and shelter. To find the families of the bereaved, to inform them and to take care of the dead and dying was his mission and his belief system. Few jobs were as well rewarded, in his view.

Between them, these two unlikely pillars of courage took it upon themselves to prepare the battered bodies in their care through the transition period between lives. They felt unworthy for the task, but they also felt compelled, moved by a force beyond their control, to not abandon the suffering victims at the crucial time of voyaging to the next life. It was their conviction. It was their custom. It was their duty.

Giving the dead the correct last ritual was not always possible. There was a permanent curfew and, whilst the Chinese authorities seemed to turn a blind eye to the collection of bodies outside the jail, burial or cremation was a high-risk strategy. The beautiful Sky Burial, where the corpse is taken to a sacred mountain, the body dismembered and cut into small pieces as an offering to the vultures, had to be adapted. The vultures did not come into the city, but there were dogs and all life deserved an offering, a last gift from the deceased.

The land in Tibet is often hard and rocky — difficult to dig at any depth — and the few trees are carefully looked after, so firewood for cremation is scarce. The practice of Sky Burial was developed in Tibet as a means to both maintain hygiene and to offer a gift to the wild animals. At the same time, it symbolised a necessary detachment from the corporeal weakness of the body.

The two men became alert. If there was a sign of life in this broken monk, then they must get him medical help. Quickly they wrapped him in an old handwoven rug. It would work as a stretcher. Time was of the essence. The monk had been thrown out as dead and it would be better if he stayed that way. If the authorities discovered him alive, they would almost certainly kill him. They staggered through the crumbling doorway and into the alley. A piece of the wooden frame came away, long untended, a sliver of faint red paint where it had been hidden from the light for a generation. It clattered to the cobblestone floor. Across the way, a neighbour became agitated at the commotion. He was Tibetan and vaguely comprehended what the two men were doing. He motioned them into his house and then straight out through the back door.

It was late. Most people were in bed, but the thin walls and congested living spaces allowed for little in the way of secrets. Quiet feet pattered around rooms, whispered conversations. Everyone instantly knew the calamity. The monk was alive.

Yes, calamity. Dead was difficult, but alive was desperately complicated. They were all Tibetans. The oppression, the pain, the suffering, all was felt equally. The monk had suffered for them all and he had to be helped and hidden at the same time. The whispers were the same at every turn in every alleyway. 'How can we help?'

The small door at the back of the hospital opened slightly and the struggling men heaved themselves through, their precious burden placed carefully on the floor. News of what was coming had already reached one particular doctor who saw the risk of treating a condemned man as little more than his duty as a human being.

The monk was breathing in desperate rasps. Struggling for breath. The gaps between inhalations becoming ever fainter, ever more apart, and the doctor pumped his chest even though he knew the ribs were smashed. Life first, treatment later. The patient, barely conscious, responded.

Quickly a bed was found and the identity of the previously deceased occupant was assumed for the incoming victim. The family would not mind. They would be happy to help one stay alive for the one they had lost. Silent grieving. Silent prayers. Silent shock. The circle of courage expanded. Everything was quickly taken care of, and when the Chinese military patrolled the Third People's Hospital of Tibet in the morning, all beds were full. All lips were sealed.

Tashi hovered between life and death for three weeks. His eye, which had been forced out of his cheek by a mighty blow to his head, was surgically replaced, but he would never see out of it again. The deep incisions on his face, his lip torn ragged from his chin, his eyebrow stuttering jaggedly across his temple, all were stitched back into place. His broken bones were splinted, but the internal injuries were severe. His body swelled up like a balloon. There was little which could be done but wait and nourish the body with little parcels of nutrients and the spirit with prayers.

At his bedside, small groups would gather daily and sit in quiet vigil. At the approach of a uniform, they would silently disperse. Someone thought they knew who he might be and his brother was summoned from far away.

Chapter 6
The Note

Outside the monastery at Drepung, the untidy group of tourists hovered between moving on and staying put. It was an interesting moral argument.

Some had guessed that moving on would be in the best interests of their increasingly forlorn-looking guide. He had plunged into despair, even forgetting to run his fingers through his defiant black hair. He struggled between beseeching the skies and beseeching the cobblestones, the nature of his hair winning the contest over style. He looked to be on the verge of crying.

Others were more interested in the fate of their companion and felt that abandoning her would be churlish, to say the least. Side conversations became debates and it was resolved to wait an hour before moving on. They would wait together outside the monastery whilst the guide gathered news from within.

Margot had been handling the situation well. In a side room off the monastery, she had acted the innocent traveller. Her hands nonchalantly in her pockets, she denied receiving anything. She assumed the manner of an imperturbable duchess and demanded in full voice to see the British Ambassador. It was a good move. The Chinese officer did not want this small local scuffle balloon into a full-scale diplomatic event. He scowled openly. He was used to having the upper hand in negotiations. He instructed a chubby-faced soldier to take Margot back to the group of tourists shuffling in the dust outside. Later, he would reflect on how he could have achieved a better outcome.

All the while, a metaphorical hole was burrowing its way through Firenza's pocket. She did not know if anyone had seen Margot's sleight of hand in passing her the note. She did not know if the note was written in a language she would understand, but she guessed it was important. Maybe it was intended for the world beyond Tibet, maybe it was local and urgent. Maybe a lot of things, but she trusted her instinct and ignored the persistent nagging in her pocket. She would look when she got back to the hotel.

Reunited, the group made for the tourist bus. A pall hung over their spirits. Something had gone wrong and they could not define it. Their guide ushered them to the steps.

Form behind them, in the monastery, there was a quick movement, muffled voices gave way to a frightened cry. One monk ran straight through the entrance doors and far into the street. There was something about him, different, amiss, troubling. He stood there, defiant, clenching his hands, head turned upwards. Then an aura of calm surrounded him. He lifted his hands, palms together, in a posture of greeting, and lowered his shaven head in supplication.

In his left hand was a matchbox. In this right hand was a match. He struck them together.

The flames leapt up from his red and yellow robes in a burst of energy, a whoosh of impatient ignition. Firenza watched in petrified horror. The outline of his smoothly shaven head filtered through the curtain of fire; eyes closed, face calm, relaxed, tranquil. She was gripped by a jarring moment of intense surrealism. It was as if he was not on fire, yet he was. She felt she was looking at the scene from a very long way away. From a great height. An observer. Detached. Maybe that was her own survival mechanism stepping in. Maybe if she had allowed herself to enter the terrible enormity of the situation, the pain he must be enduring, the factors which had pushed him to this, the very nature of the air she was breathing, or maybe not breathing, she would feel that to breathe was almost an affront to the nature of this act. It was as if the entire planet was standing still, inhaling but unable to exhale. Paralysis. Even the leaves on the pine trees could not bring themselves to rustle for shock, even perhaps for respect.

Why wasn't anyone rushing to put out the flames? Why was everyone staring, rooted to the spot? She didn't know what to do. She wanted to stop it, yet it was mesmerising. A young monk, calmly standing in the middle of a street, in the middle of a silent prayer, on fire.

It was already too late. The monk, his head tilted slightly to one side, seemed to convey the gentlest demeanour, almost of peace, of silent compassion. The mildest of smiles played at the corners of his mouth and he fell gently to his knees, surrounded by a sheath of translucent flames of gold and amber and rose. He slowly sat back on his heels and the consuming flames rushed and multiplied. They crackled and shrank his skin and clothing, charring them black. Firenza was still staring in horror at his face, as the yellow-orange of the flames licked as if in a lover's passion. She looked on transfixed as the face slowly lost its features. Nose, eyes, mouth, ears, seemed to blend and dissolve. Not once did that face show pain. Nor utter a single cry. The young monk passed in the yellow flames from life to death with immaculate dignity.

Tearing her focus away, Firenza looked at the few onlookers. The tourists hung on to each other in shared horror. The Tibetans stood around, heads bowed, in silent respect, in sadness, in understanding. They knew why. This was the ultimate act of helpless defiance. A desperate plea to the world beyond the mountains of Tibet.

It had happened before, so many times. Too many times. It was the only instrument of protest they had. This spectacular suicide. This mix of fatalistic and altruistic suicide. The act of self-immolation had been used as an effective instrument of protest over and over again. It was political protest in extremis.

Firenza and the others stayed where they were, too shocked to move. Even their guide had given up all pretence of cover-up. They had witnessed an uncanny mode of power. The onlookers had been given agency and the baton of action had been silently transferred from the smouldering remains of a nameless monk to the motley crew of internationals mutely gathered at the spectacle. Had they but known it, they now had a particular job to do. The message had been clear. 'What will you do now you have seen this?'

They were gathered up and ushered quickly away by their hapless guide, himself sick with worry and verging on speechless. Firenza glanced back at the smouldering remains of the monk. Black, angular bone, in a blackened patch of cobblestones in a blackened world. She wondered if he was dead now. She hoped he was. It was agony to think otherwise. Who would know? Who would care? The world was not looking. There was no press. No media, no witness of any note.

Firenza cared. She cared in a helpless, shameful way. Maybe none of it was her fault. Maybe all of it was her fault. Her horror at witnessing the smouldering, fuming and dying human body was slowly being transformed to disgust at the political culture responsible for such a terrible sight.

The journey back to the Himalayan Yak Hotel passed in silence. The weight of witness was heavy. Somebody rustled a packet of sweets and it felt like an affront to the dead.

Their guide, mustering the last vestiges of authority about his person announced, "Due to the unfortunate incident of this morning, we will meet here in the lobby in one hour where the chief of police will address us." The hair was now hanging limply around his face. He made one half-hearted attempt to push it back before collapsing hopelessly in an armchair. His thoughts were morose. How he could expect to have a future in the tourist industry after today was beyond his reasoning capabilities. He would try and retrieve the situation as best he could, but in these harsh political times, he knew his family would have to suffer — one way or another.

Margot steered Firenza through the small lobby. "Come and have a cup of tea in my room. It will calm us." She said this rather loudly so that everyone could hear.

Firenza had not forgotten about the note and, fortunately, any discomfort she had about keeping it hidden had diminished with the onslaught to her senses brought on by the morning's events. She wished it didn't exist. Her senses told her it would bring trouble — or, at the very least, complications — so it was with foreboding reluctance that she accompanied Margot to her room.

"Can I see that note now?" said Margot as soon as the door was closed.

Firenza groped in her pocket. In her haste, she had just stuffed it in like a used tissue. Out it came, crinkled and torn.

She began to straighten it out with her fingers. Teasing the corners straight with the edge of her nails.

"Hold on a minute," said Margot. "Let's do it gently so as not to smudge it or miss anything important."

Firenza put it on the table. They peered at it. Just a piece of scrunched up pale blue paper, thick and rough — a bit like old blotting paper, with some scribbles on it.

Margot gently teased the folds apart. The letters were difficult to read, but they were in a kind of English. The chances were that it had been written by a Tibetan in broken English.

"Do you think they were expecting us?" said Firenza.

"Who knows. Most tourists coming here speak at least some English. Maybe we were the catalyst for that awful scene."

Firenza didn't like to think she was in any way responsible, but she understood what Margot was saying. It would be futile to commit such a desperate act if the only witnesses had been Tibetans with little recourse to the outside world.

They studied the writing. It was thin and curly, uneven and unfinished. It had obviously been written in a hurry or under great pressure. The two women discussed the words, and what the intended meaning might be. They finally agreed that it said:

I Dorjee Wangdu
I monk at Labrang Monastery
Chinese want destroy Tibetan life Destroy monastery Destroy monks.
Very much torture. Very much sadness
Please tell world General Li Enlai very bad man.
Kill many nuns and monks.
I give life you stop him. Life for Free Tibet

Firenza and Margot sat in a long silence.

"I took a picture," said Margot reluctantly.

Firenza was shocked. How could she? A man was burning to death and she took a picture of it?

"I know," said Margot, reading her thoughts. "It was weird, but the camera was in my hand and I just clicked a couple of times. I had this feeling that I should be a good witness. I knew it was a desperate political act. These things have happened many times before in this country."

Firenza argued with herself over the morality or lack of it. She had been frozen to the spot as the young monk burned, so she could hardly lay claim to any moral high ground.

"Look," continued Margot, "we might be searched and have our stuff confiscated. If that poor man was to have died for anything at all, we must try and get this to the world outside Tibet. You see what it's like here. Everything is controlled. If we can't get the photos out of this country, his death would be for nothing."

Firenza nodded, her brain struggling on the fringes of understanding. "Happened many times before?"

Margot ignored her. "The internet connection is down. Possibly because of us. I'm going to photograph this note and then transfer the pictures to your phone." Then as an afterthought, "With your permission. Bluetooth?"

Firenza had no idea how to argue. She offered her phone to Margot.

"Have you got a memory card?"

Firenza nodded. It was all becoming bit of a dream.

"Now, when the transfer is complete, take the memory card out and hide it as well as you can. The lining of your sponge bag, for example. Go back to your room now. Take a rest. We'll have to go downstairs again in half an hour."

Firenza dragged her feet down the sparse corridor of the Himalayan Yak Hotel. She wanted to sleep it all away, but first, she took her mobile phone apart and removed the SD card. She walked around the room with the tiny piece of data memory between her finger and thumb. So small, yet so big. The obvious places to hide it — like the lining of her suitcase — seemed to be more fitting to a cops and robbers movie, and she quailed at the thought of someone finding it in such an obvious place. She wondered if it would show up in an X-ray.

Well, she couldn't know. It would depend on the sensitivity of the scanner. Should she hide it inside her bra? Or maybe deep in her wallet? She dithered for an eternity.

Oh, she wanted desperately to sleep, but she had to think. Leaving it in her hotel room could be high risk. It might be searched. She dug through her suitcase for her never-before-used Swiss Army knife. It was a present from her best friend a couple of years before, and Firenza had only packed it as an afterthought, thinking that at least the corkscrew function might be useful. Such frivolous thoughts were far from her mind now. She grappled with the stiff action on the scissors function, breaking a nail in the process, and snipped a little hole in her slightly padded bra. The memory card slipped inside, and she shimmied it down further between the lining and the lace so that it would not fall out.

Jacket pulled over her face, she lay stiffly on the bed. Confused images clouded the troubled mind she was trying to clear. Half of her knew exactly what she had seen, the other half was in denial. No matter how hard she tried to fool herself that it was a dream, she knew it wasn't. She kept seeing the face of the monk. The flames, the innate nobility in his demeanour. Why? This was the thing troubling her most. She needed to understand the note better. The words were not clear to her, or at least the meaning was not clear. She couldn't remember that Chinese name, the general. Her body shuddered. Was this man so evil that it was worth dying to get the information to a tourist?

A knock at the door. Firenza mentally pushed it away. Another knock. It was time to go downstairs. Firenza felt like a wreck. She hadn't smoothed her hair, her clothes were crumpled and she could barely walk straight, but to the lobby she went.

The other travellers were silently gathered. Their guide came in having herded together the last of their group. They were visibly wilted. The woman with the poodle hair was the most wilted of all. Gone was the perky smile and flighty bright eyes. Her hair had drooped to an inconsistent straggle.

Won Wangdu, his hairstyle slightly, only slightly, retrieved, bade them sit. It seemed that was the last thing everyone wanted to do, but he cajoled, they sat. Firenza sat on the arm of a spindly chair to avoid having to actually relax. Margot sat across the room in an upright chair. They avoided eye contact, as if to make any contact at all would be an admission of guilt, for they both knew that the note should have been handed over to the authorities, and if they were found in possession of such a thing, great suspicion would surround them, and they would probably be sent home at the first opportunity, maybe worse. Probably worse.

The hotel manager came in, accompanied by a policeman, his hat firmly on his head, his jacket immaculately pressed, buttons shining.

He addressed the room in perfect English. "My apologies to you all. You have witnessed an unfortunate incident. The person concerned is reported to have some mental health difficulties and this, we believe, is the cause of such a mishap."

'Mishap?' thought Firenza, determined not to say anything, but compelled to think much.

The policeman, who was probably of some senior rank, continued. "In order for our investigations to be completed, it is necessary for each of you to be interviewed and to make a statement for us. We will take you in alphabetical order. The hotel manager has kindly lent us his office for this purpose."

There was a general hum of understanding. Firenza wondered what had happened to the Tibetan witnesses. She wondered what had happened to the body of the monk. Most of all she wondered what to do about that note, that general, and how her part in this was going to unfold.

Chapter 7
The Monk
A Year Passes

The dreamlike backdrop of the misty mountains, pinkish-yellow in the sunrise, beautiful and deadly, a mystic religion unto themselves, soared like fantastical gods over the high plateau of Tibet.

One lone man walked slowly through the deep snow, rags binding what warmth there was to his feet. A small black dot in the blinding white. Over his shoulder was a cloth bag. In the bag were some rations of flat bread and dried yak cheese. His head and body were covered in rough furs of marmot and fox. He walked with purpose and disappeared behind a rocky outcrop. There was much on his mind, this day.

He had collected the food, as he did every week or so, from his aunt, who lived in a small village far below. His days passed in meditation, thought and prayer. Slowly his body was recovering from the injuries and the crisp mountain air imbibed him with a gradually increasing health and vigour.

The monk was in hiding. He was supposed to be dead. He had left hospital long before he was well enough to walk. But he had to leave for the sake of the doctors and nurses who were shielding him from the authorities. He had been lifted from safe house to safe house, always in danger of being discovered, but always getting a little stronger. Many Tibetans had quietly and willingly shared the burden of nursing the monk who should be dead. It was their duty and their pleasure. Over time he had been moved across the country to the rural grasslands of the east where most of his family still lived. The journey had taken a year.

He learned that his mother had died whilst he was in prison. It had been a bitter blow. No more would he feel the kindly warmth of his mother. No more would he hear her voice, feel her love, hear her guidance. He mourned the fact that he could not have been beside her, and blessed her, and paved the way to her passing to the next life. The burden of losing his mother weighed heavier than any other and would do all his life.

But his aunt stepped silently into the role of parent. Tashi had surprised them all by almost getting back to his former physical strength. For a monk, he was unusually powerful in build, unusually strong in constitution, unusually tough in every physical way. No doubt these attributes were the entire reason for his miraculous recovery, and the whispers around the village were as triumphant as they were hushed. But his arm still twitched uncontrollably and he could not control his bladder or his bowels, such was the nature of his torture and the extent of his injuries.

It was too dangerous for him to live with his aunt. The Chinese kept a rigorous note of everyone who lived in Tibet and their every movement. It would not take them long to hear about an extra mouth to feed in the area, even though the geography of the Amdo region, and the remoteness of the little village, made inspections rare. They would take a lot longer to hear about a hermit in the mountains, but hear about him they did, and the whispers ran across the mountains and the stony paths in advance of the troops, and the aunt was warned.

His only option was to live in the hills outside the village. Sometimes a neighbour brought him food, sometimes he visited his aunt. He set up a little den in one of the many hidden caves not too far from a mountain stream, but even this was too dangerous in the long term. He needed to leave Tibet.

Night after night, for those who would see, little strands of humanity left remote villages and headed for the high mountain passes. The preparation for these voyages sometimes took years. It depended upon what age a child would be judged strong enough to make the twenty-six-night mountain crossing.

Sometimes they were five years old. It was difficult, but by no means impossible, to hide a child from birth onwards. They had to avoid the annual census. They had to avoid being seen. They had to avoid school. In the distant provinces, such desperate sleight of hand was possible. Maybe a still-birth would be recorded and the healthy baby smuggled to another family for a few nights. Maybe they just got lucky. Either way, the desperate task of continuing their culture was imperative. No Tibetan family could be sure their child would not be seized by the Chinese authorities and sent to China for 'education', never to be heard of again, and such was the love for the Dalai Lama and his kindly authority, that to risk their children in such a terrible journey was thought to be the only worthwhile gift to their future.

On rare occasions the parents went with the child, resting only for a night or two before retracing their steps across the frozen peaks. If they were found missing, the repercussions on the remaining family would be harsh. The punishment was incarceration or death and who could tell which was worse.

In response to this constant trickling of humanity from across the highest and most inhospitable mountain range in the world, the Tibetan Government-in-Exile had set up orphanages and schools for thousands of children in North India, and for sixty years the trickle had remained constant, the faith never wavering, the torment which drove them never abating.

The month was October. In the shortening days, plans were discussed and preparations made. Small huddles of people started to gather at various outposts along the mountainous border with Nepal. Tashi collected food and drink from well-wishers. It was woefully inadequate for the journey. His aunt gave him her most precious possession — an amber necklace — and he set off with a small child from the village, a teenager from the district, and a nun, to find the guide they had been told about. They had very little money, inappropriate clothing, and no map.

The journey would be across many hundreds of miles of mountainous passes. It would take months. None of them knew the way. They were born in the mountains, had mountain instincts, but they did not know where they were going, and they did not know how. They only knew that their final destination was the Dalai Lama's home in the colonially named McLeod Ganj, nestling in a cleft of the mountains above Dharamshala, Northern India. Little Lhasa, they called it.

Chapter 8
The Mountains

None of the fleeing travellers had heard much in the way of stories from those who had survived the journey across the highest mountain range in the world to Kathmandu. There were rumours of course. But those who had made it were inclined to try and forget the ordeal and did not divulge much. Those who did not make it kept their stories buried with them, in the snow, if they were lucky, for the journey from Tibet into Nepal is a treacherous one, fraught with physical and mental hardships and egregious violations of basic human rights. You did not want to be caught by Chinese soldiers along the way; their reputation for cruelty was probably the only thing anyone knew for sure. But apart from that, precious little news filtered back from either the refugee camps in Nepal or any Tibetans who had successfully made it to northern India. The traffic across these frontiers was almost always one way.

Tashi had first taken a selection of buses to get him closer to the border between Tibet and Nepal. The wide grasslands and sacred lakes of emerald and topaz slowly gave way to boulders the size of a house. Overhead, birds of blue and russet and black, and pink, their extraordinary calls drowned out by the rasping engine of human invention, eked out their living on the gifts of the land. Green-necked ducks bobbed for fish and the tiny rose-finches sat upon the pine trees singing to the sky. Occasionally the buff-necked spectacle of a huge Himalayan vulture stood sunning itself on a rocky crag, or groups of them wheeled overhead, the fingers of their wing feathers ruffling in the breeze as they patiently awaited their next meal. And all the while the mountains grew closer, taller, darker.

He no longer travelled as a monk; it would draw too much attention. He did not know if the authorities had reached the village of his aunt, or if they even suspected his existence. He did know that the whispering grapevine was usually correct and he worried for the kind aunt he had inadvertently put into danger, for the Chinese authorities were ruthless in exacting punishment on transgressors. In menacing contrast to the Buddhist philosophy of the region, there was little in the way of compassion shown to the indigenous population. You could be shot in the street for walking whilst being Tibetan.

The buses were a mediocre affair of accidents waiting to happen. These were not the smooth-running tourist buses of lavish seating and air conditioning. They were run down, dusty and barely roadworthy heaps of battered metal, teetering on the brink of scrappage. The roads were often just glorified tracks and they wound crazily through the mountains without a care. On one side was the ubiquitous drop of nightmares, on the other a wall of bare rock, protuberances set at just the right height to make you want to duck or squirm or both. The drivers had less care than the roads, playing popular tinny music at full volume, turning round to have protracted jocular conversations with the people behind and rotating the wheel madly in one direction and then the other, whilst not appearing to cast even half an eye at the road they were travelling. Health and safety weren't even the stuff of distant legend. No one had heard of it. Thus, neither passengers nor driver showed the least concern at their regularly approaching demise, which tended to fade away as soon as it appeared. They knew better than to worry about matters outside of their control.

The journey to the border between Tibet and Nepal was more than two thousand miles long. They were slow, rough, difficult miles. For a while, they travelled alongside the snaking upper reaches of the lazy Mekong River as they left Chamdo. The mountains loomed bare and snow-capped on either side. Settlements were few and opportunities to buy food and drink sparse. The travellers wrapped their animal skin coats around them and settled down to pass the time as pleasantly as they could. Between them they shared everything, taking special care of the little ones. The narrow riverbed was now all there was to cultivate crops in any meaningful way. Small fields of potatoes, banked up against the cold, ran in strips across the valley. It wasn't time to harvest yet, but already the hardy qingke barley was poking heads of green through the rocky soil.

Rarely without a toothy smile, Tashi struck up conversations with all who sat near. Taking care to be non-committal about his origins, he made a huge fuss about the children travelling with them. He joked and played and laughed. By contrast, the nun, who was about his age, remained silent. Hair still very short, she could not disguise who she was. She neither smiled nor conversed. She only nodded at times when food or drink was offered and silently accepted these offerings with eyes of watery blue. Tashi gave her all the space she needed. He didn't question her. He knew the nuns had a hard time at the hands of the Chinese. Often retiring by nature, Tibetan females kept themselves as far as possible from the gaze of the soldiers. Many nuns lived in distant convents in the mountains, rarely went out, and spent their days studying and tending to their gardens and their cows. It was a double horror to them if the soldiers broke into their fragile environment. Those that could, hid. The beatings and rapes were not spoken of, they had to be accepted. There was no recourse to the law when the law was the guilty party. The nuns needed only to look into each other's eyes to know the damage inflicted on their cloistered lives and violated bodies. They avoided eye contact with other people. Often their pain ran too close to the surface and they preferred to keep it behind closed doors.

The child in their care was five years old. She was ruddy-cheeked and hearty. Clearly her family had taken care to build her up physically for the journey. It had probably been planned since her birth. She had three siblings and a loving family. The tears at their separation had been pitiful, for whilst there was always some hope that the family might be reunited, in practice, and under the current repressive occupation, it would be impossible. Her mother, so torn between giving her daughter a better life and wanting her to stay, tried to find the strength to stick to the prescribed plan of less emotional goodbyes.

The parting, this final parting, this tearing of the heart, this crushing loss, it was more than a mother could bear. To say goodbye, forever, to your daughter of just five years, no matter how carefully planned, no matter the rehearsals, no matter the good intention, the point of actual physical termination was too much for rational thought. At the last minute, the simple peasant mother crumpled physically, her head in her hands, desperately fighting herself to retain control and losing the battle pathetically, irrevocably. She broke down and wailed pitifully, her misery lying raw and open like a weeping wound. If it was possible to bleed tears, the streets would be running red with her blood. Veering uncontrollably between what she should do and what she could not help doing, did not make it easier for her child, who despite having been told what was in store for her, could not comprehend what it really meant.

Little Dekyi, reflecting the stress and confusion in her mother, wailed in unison, her small ruddy face a tear-streaked wilderness of bewilderment. The parting was messy and emotional. Eventually, her father agreed to walk some of the way with his daughter to form a softer emotional bridge. The walk was more than twenty rugged miles. He laid her sleepy little frame tenderly on the seat of the bus, and the physical parting was complete. The emotional parting would never be complete.

Tenzin, the teenager, was fortunately from a large and loving family. He had all manner of tricks and diversions with which to entertain a small child. Deyki took his hand willingly when they walked off to find breakfast on the first morning and the two of them struck up a rapport of comfort, for he too would miss his family, and in the dark cold nights on the mountain, the two of them could be found curled and snuggled together like father and child, sister and brother.

Many of the people they encountered on their journey suspected what they were about, but never a word was said. Food and drink were offered in every village they passed, as is the Tibetan custom, and Tashi, a monk whose life of meditation and learning had been so brutally interrupted, still could not hide the modest and bowing demeanour of his order. He was probably the worst disguised, if you discounted the nun, for apart from the local travellers, there were probably others secretly seeking sanctuary. He accepted the offerings of nourishment as became a holy man, bowing and giving blessings. He couldn't help himself. And so, they travelled, sometimes walking, sometimes accepting a lift, always accepting the food offered by simple villagers along the way, whose need was almost the same as theirs. The poorest of the world know what it is to go without and, paradoxically, offer the most help to others.

The little band of four did not stop long anywhere. They slept where they could in houses, under walls, in monasteries and makeshift tents. It was imperative to make the journey before winter set in. If the depth of snow did not kill them, the wind chill certainly would.

One bus journey followed another, and another, and so on until they reached the places where buses could not go and the chattering diminished to a hush. From now on they would be at the mercy of the weather and the mountains. The clouds loomed in front of them. Ominously piling their grey load ever higher upon the mountains. Tashi prayed for a late winter, but the heavens threatened otherwise.

They climbed higher, leaving the patches of green in the valleys below, and taking the stony road to traverse the tops of the lower mountains as they had been told. They could not stop at the major monasteries along the route, because here there were often tourists and that meant they were policed by the Chinese. Yet all along the rough road there were people who sent word of their passing, and from time to time there were parcels of food left for refugee travellers such as they. Dried cheese, dried yak meat and the flat and nourishing barley bread. Drink was no problem as the mountain streams ran clear and cool, high enough to be unpolluted by industry and the mucky detritus of humanity.

They washed their clothes in these streams, shaking out the dust and sweat of the journeying and banging the cloth against the stones. For Tashi, these mountain streams brought moments of unabated liberty. Despite their coldness, he would lie in them for as long as he could stand, letting the glacial waters run over him, imagining their frozen source high in the mountains, feeling the crisp purity wash away his struggles, for Tashi was still doubly incontinent. His body had never completely recovered from the torture. He knew he could not hide his troubles, though he never stopped being embarrassed, sitting for long hours on buses had been tribulation, public accidents did happen, sometimes he never seemed to stop apologising. In many ways, he was glad to be travelling on foot and at a pace he was comfortable with. There were few accidents, and anyway, they were familiar enough with each other to laugh about the situation with him and give him the privacy he needed when wet patches appeared on his trousers. It was never going to be a comfortable journey for Tashi, but life does not always deal good choices and he travelled with the sustaining optimism that his condition could one day be cured. Maybe he could get to England. He heard that there were very good doctors in England and, in his strange haphazard way, that is where he set his sights.

Occasionally a group of monks would meet them along the way. They would help to carry little Deyki on their backs, for sturdy as she was, her legs could only take her so far. The monks would give directions to the next place of safety and shelter, and in this way, they travelled in the footsteps of the thousands who had gone before them. So passed the days and weeks like the fluttering prayer flags dotted around the landscape on piles of weathered stone. The waypoints had stood for centuries. The brutal winds tearing at the colourful fabric, the piercing sun bleaching the printed mantras until they faded away to the universe. Tired and footsore, the tiny band marched on and the weather held fine.

They skirted Lhasa city by a wide margin and were joined by more would-be refugees. Two young men, friends from a remote village, and an older woman who reminded Tashi of his aunt. She was called Jetsun and Tashi took it upon himself to look after her as if she was indeed his relative. He fussed over her, made sure she always had food, even if it was his, and generally became her self-appointed protector.

Jetsun took these offerings of goodwill in the spirit in which they were intended. In truth, she was a well-established teacher with a significant following, but knew she was in danger of arrest. Her home was in the east of Tibet, only a few hundred miles from where

Tashi was born, and they chatted amicably as they walked the pitted road. Jetsun did not give Tashi or anyone else her real name. It was prudent of her, for the grapevine of whispers sometimes worked both ways — for you and against you — and her leaving would be quickly noticed, no matter the false trail she had laid in other directions.

At a monastery in the high foothills of the Himalayas, the straggly band of six stopped to gather their strength. It was an awesome sight, the one they had been aiming at for more than one thousand miles. The last monastery. The monastery of legend. Lofka.

They paused at the whitewashed entrance, arched and adorned with the painted details of blue and red and gold, and rested a little on the ground.

Bright prayer flags fluttered in the breeze and, as they looked up, they could see the monastic buildings perched impossibly high up on the rocky crags. Some were newly whitewashed, some were crumbling away, yet each found a teetering foothold on the steep brown cliffs.

Tashi had heard about this impossible place from other monks in another life. The life before prison. The microscopic life of learning and tranquillity he had almost forgotten, yet here he was, in the reality of the stories long told, surveying the soaring buildings as they hugged the high bare rocks and defied the work of God and gravity.

Chapter 9
The Dawning of Truth

Firenza was not even dimly aware that her life was going to change irrevocably. The immolation, the note, the heightened awareness of the politics of this region, had all seemed like just another challenge thrown at her in a life in which challenge was seldom passed over. Immensely difficult though it all was, she thought she would only have to find a way to process it, then get back to her apartment and her job and let life continue.

But it wouldn't.

The burning of the monk could not be filed away like hang gliding — as part of an adventure holiday. The image never left her. It became her motivation. Her calling. Her inspiration. In this way, the young monk had not died in vain. Firenza fought for a while to let her everyday brain push the idea away, but something in her was stronger. It just came fizzling to the top whenever she stopped concentrating on suppressing it. The thought was outside her experience, yet it seemed to be intrinsic to her every fibre. Justice. She wanted justice. She wanted it for all the tired ruddy-cheeked Tibetans who were suffering under such an inhumane regime.

She would take the note and the pictures home with her, she would go to the media and she would give eyewitness testimony, and she would tell all who would listen what was happening in Tibet. She would research and she would learn more. She would seek out Li Enlai somehow and find ways to deal with him. She, a young woman in her twenties would do all this and, armed with the fortitude and ignorance of youth, made her decision.

The only outstanding matter was how.

The holiday continued. The itinerary was not interrupted again. Firenza knew she was being watched from a distance, but continued to act as if she was not. Her unlikely partnership with Margot ripened and, whenever they could steal an hour or so on their own, she would ply Margot with questions. The answers inevitably led to even more questions and by the end of the second week, Firenza had amassed a mountain of information — not all of which she truly understood, but which she stored in her brain for future reference.

It seemed that no one else had seen the passing of the note in the Lebrang monastery, but there was clear suspicion among the authorities. The two women concluded that using the internet might be a big risk and could therefore delay their return home. It was tricky being in the midst of a paradox. On the one hand, they had a terrible news story that could be taken up by several media outlets immediately. On the other, the very act of trying to disseminate the story could cause it to be suffocated. The final argument against sending it was that maybe no one would use the story at all as it interfered with the politics of the country involved. They could be detained as political prisoners for trying to 'traffic' the information.

As it was, they were determined to smuggle out the pictures and the note. Abandoning the quest was to make that poor monk's death worse than useless.

Margot knew well enough that Britain was in the process of targeting China as a major trading partner, despite its appalling human rights record. She was wily enough to know that major organs such as the BBC would not carry the story for political reasons, but she did not tell Firenza. Firenza would have to learn the degree of hypocrisy prevalent in the news cycle for herself. Britain was not interested in human rights. It was only interested in Chinese markets, cheap goods and finance.

On their penultimate day, the so-called holidaymakers were allowed to wander a little in the small streets close to the hotel. Firenza sensed she was being trailed. Her discreet shadow was a diminutive Chinese woman, dressed in mid-grey trousers and a darker grey jacket. She seemed young, but there again many Chinese women looked young to Firenza, at least until they looked very old, which seemed to happen suddenly. It was something to do with the head to body proportions. Often with their narrow shoulders and small bodies, they would appear to Firenza as children or even toddlers. It was sometimes hard not to think of them as dolls. Their alabaster faces contrasted strongly with the fresh ruddy-cheeked look of most Tibetans. Tibetan women, men and children were robust in build, relished eye contact and smiled a lot. The difference between the two contrasted strongly enough for Firenza to know the difference. There was also an indefinable air about her shadowy companion. She knew how to blend into a wall, a tree, anything, yet it was this very ability of knowing how to blend in which marked her out as different. It was almost as if her lack of appearance, her lack of smell, lack of aura, announced her presence.

Gathering as much nonchalance as she could, Firenza poked about the little shops, bowing and repeating the ubiquitous greeting 'Tashi Dalek' as often as possible. Her budget was tiny and she had reserved her last day for buying mementos. She let her shadow follow her on a zigzag through the narrow alleyways, but unfortunately, she meandered close to a small monastery and so she unwittingly entered the realm of the ancient monk.

He was sitting in a chair, dozing slightly, but mischievously alert at the same time. Firenza crept past on her way to look at the paintings on the wall. She had previously been drawn to the Green Tara and even from the doorway, she could spot a version of the female deity painted large and fading on the monastery wall. One of their guides had, in response to her question, given some background information, and it had chimed with something deep inside her and invoked a sense of universal bond.

The Green Tara was a kind of Buddhist deity. Firenza had long been drawn to the colour green. It was the colour of growth and regeneration, and life itself, and evoked in her the sense of a natural healthy world. A few days ago, the guide Wen Wangdu had told her that this Tara was also the symbol of healing, the release of fear and ignorance. He had explained that human ignorance comes in many forms — jealousy and pride being principle among them — and the healing energy of the Green Tara brings awareness and relief from these negative characteristics.

It was a thought worth pondering in a mind as open as Firenza's, so it was with some familiarity that she stood before the beautifully painted Tara, resplendent in her green skin amongst the mandala of figurative countryside and complex animal symbolism.

The old monk opened both eyes. He was shrinking and huddled in his maroon robes, wrapped tight as a baby against the cold, but his eyes shone brightly amidst their nest of many wrinkles.

"Ah. Green Tara, you like." It was less of a question, more of a statement. He nodded happily as if she had already answered in the affirmative. "Human mind is complex and profound. She bring you peace if you want her to."

Firenza smiled at him, a little bit of a loss as to how she had entered a conversation without saying a word.

Maybe he had a special relationship with the Green Tara himself, because he seemed to rise a little higher in his chair and become more bodily animated without actually moving a limb. "She will help with doubts that disturb the mind. If you want her to. Internal dangers are like external dangers. Same difference."

Firenza nodded, though she wasn't exactly sure at what. His endearing face enticed her to cast a smile at him and she couldn't help herself smiling back.

She looked again at the painting of the Green Tara, then glanced at the doorway through which the bright light of day was silhouetting the figure of her Chinese shadow. Internal and external. Doubts on both sides. Self-doubt. Doubt about the future. Doubt about even being able to get on the plane. She looked again at the monk who was still smiling at her. There was love in that smile.

"Thank you," she said. "Tashi delek."

"Keep her image with you. Here," he said, finally announcing that he had a limb by uncovering an arm and pointing with one brown finger to his temple. Then he huddled back down into himself, and slowly, peacefully closed his eyes, the gentle smile still upon his face.

Firenza took one last look at the Tara and reluctantly turned away. She did not know which image would remain the stronger, the Tara or the old monk. It would have been nice to stay peacefully beside him for a while and erase the image of the burning monk which was permanently imprinted on the surface of her mind, but she had a job to do. Maybe by fulfilling that mission, the image would fade, but, for now, there was tourist shopping to do and a spook to entertain.

The following day would be the day of their departure. She and Margot had arranged not to be too close to each other in the run up to the journey. They had already made plans for the airport, for customs, for security, and Margot had made even more plans than Firenza knew, just to be sure.

Ironically, it was a relief to be leaving. Tibet should have been a gifted adventure, instead, it had become a catalyst for anxiety and more knowledge than Firenza felt she needed. In a few short hours, her life had turned upside down. Turning it back was not going to be possible, yet she would try to fool herself for a while longer.

She took a last look at the high mountains which framed the Tibetan plateau, their snowy peaks inhospitable, yet enticing, and her eyes followed down to the windswept slopes where herders tended their shaggy yaks. In her mind, she could still recall the rough metal bells clonking at their necks. It was a relaxing pastoral sound, though she doubted the yaks thought as much. She recalled the ruddy red cheeks of the Tibetan people, their open faces and ready smiles and knew the visit had left its mark in her psyche. The land was harsh and beautiful. It had tried to speak to her in its unrelentingly spiritual way and Firenza had tried to listen. She had watched the soaring birds, sat beside the jewelled waters of the lakes and listened to the monks in quiet prayer.

Through the prism of the burning monk, Firenza felt an overwhelming need to protect this country and its beleaguered people, and she set herself against the sudden chill wind and walked to the coach which was to take her to the next level of destiny, scarf flying its primary colours in flamboyant defiance of her thoughtful mood and all who might stop her in her quest.

Chapter 10
The Himalayas

They were expected. A young monk scrabbled down the rocky path to meet them, bowing a profuse welcome before he even came to a halt. He had a steel flask of precious water in his hand, which he offered to the tired visitors. He explained, apologetically, that climate change had decreased the amount of snowfall in recent years and the streams and rivulets on which the high monastery depended for water were diminished, so they could not offer baths or showers right now.

The little party bowed back in greeting. They each took less water than they needed.

The young monk led them up the path towards the monastery entrance. The familiar Himalayan archway, with its snow-white walls and painted motifs of red and gold, stood solid against the world, the weather and all comers. The unknown design hand of these walls and all within reached back before memory. It reached back beyond Buddhism to the ancient places of learning. Often these motifs were born from caves, where isolated monks would meditate in the calmness of a natural world. The subsequent sculptors and engineers of two thousand years past took great pride in their work. They honed their skills on isolated plateaux and bare cliffs. Their beautiful adornments of colour defied time itself and, with deep respect, their tradition was carried forward, maintained, and reborn.

The travellers removed their shoes and entered the courtyard. Across the well-worn stone floor was the entrance to the main temple, but they were led aside to a modest hall of clay walls and floor, where a simple table of bread and cheese was laid out for them. An urn of Tibetan tea promised welcome warmth and the salty yak butter infusion promised essential energy and comfort in the cold thin air.

Neither Tashi nor his companions had ever admitted to being hungry and little Deyki had no need to be hungry because there was always food for her, even if the others had to go without.

Monks from the monastery came to join them at the wooden table. They did not eat. Indeed, it was possible to imagine that the food the travellers were eating was their food, but it was not polite to mention it. The travellers needed to eat as well as they could because the long cold journey in front of them would inevitably waste their bodies. The monks of Lofka knew all this and would give everything they had, many times over, to minimise the suffering of the journey ahead.

Mealtimes were a robust form of joy. Those sitting around the table would exchange stories and make each other rock with glee. In almost the same breath they would lean forward and impart tales of excruciating sadness until their heads dropped in near despair, then without warning something funny would be said and they would rock back in uncontrived peals of laughter. It was the Tibetan way, not to take, even in conversation, until you can give more. Thus, the inevitable sadness of the loss of their country and their culture, their friends and families, would be balanced with light-hearted stories and slapstick jokes. Always balance. Mental and physical, in the oldest tradition in the world.

The little nun ate timidly and sparingly; the rest of them knew it was their duty to eat well. Tashi cast a sidelong glance at Jetsun. It was quite probable that the nun had suffered extreme torture, and very likely multiple rapes, before she joined them. It was common for nuns to be raped by Chinese soldiers if they were caught. Sometimes monks were forced to publicly rape nuns. There was no end to the indignity. The nun was clearly suffering a deep inner sadness, but all attempts to coax more than a syllable out of her had been met with disappointment. Barely a smile had crossed her face in all the weeks they had travelled together, yet she walked on doggedly beside them, silently, a ghost whose spirit had been stolen.

The sun stayed kind, though it was November, and the travellers helped out wherever they could, gathering wood — of which there was little — tending the gardens, lifting the potatoes which, together with the barley already harvested, would be their main source of carbohydrates over the winter, and packing them into the dark dry cellars under the dwelling spaces of the monastery.

One week was enough. They were rested and needed to start the most challenging part of the journey — the high mountains of snow, and wind, and ice. To think about it was one thing, to take the first real step was another.

As they left the main gateway, one of the older monks came out to say goodbye. Across his arms lay an oblong package, wrapped in orange cloth. Tashi recognised, almost without having to think, what was being asked of him. The two monks smiled a gentle, painful smile to each other, and the package was transferred delicately from the older monk to Tashi.

Inside would be the holy books of ancient times, more than one thousand years old. Diligently copied by hands long passed, by the light of butter-wax candles in the cold Tibetan winters. Holy texts and prayers, which might have stayed in Lofka monastery for another thousand years, were being dispersed. All knew that Lofka would not remain forever intact. Remote that it was, the contents would one day be forcibly taken and burned, like so many others.

Tashi opened his travelling sack and took out some food. There was no other way to accommodate the holy books. The tough road ahead would need both hands free for climbing and helping others. Tashi's smile was genuine. It was a great honour. The two monks bowed to each other in mutual understanding. The others stood by in silence. The sacrifice was great, but they were Tibetans. They understood. Their country might be lost, but they would do whatever it took to make sure their culture survived. The Chinese had yet to learn that the more you oppressively stamp on a people, the more they stubbornly root to their culture.

And so, the road, which was not a road, spread out before them. Soon they would have to travel by night only, heading south-west, their guides the stars.

Refreshed, they strode out, trying not to dwell on the craggy snow line in front of them and the high peaks beyond, thankfully lost in cloud for now, because to see them would be to cast doubt on their ability as mere mortals to complete the journey. Their guide, a young monk who had done this only once before, and returned physically unscathed, did not relish the job. He had made it to the Nepalese border intact, but not all of his troop had. The stories he had never told were written on his face and he did not relish another journey. But he was asked, and so volunteered.

For two days they tripped and climbed the boulder-strewn patches of bare earth just below the snowline, keeping to the cliffs, pausing behind the most promising shelter. To be seen at this stage would make the journey of the past few months futile, so a labouring silence transmitted itself between the travellers. By day three, little Deyki was having to be carried some of the way and Jetsun, the one who reminded Tashi of his aunt, was labouring hard. The nun, for whom silence was a chosen state, used it to keep a wall around her, maybe to keep out something dark, maybe silence was her shield. She ate silently, walked silently, prayed silently. Sometimes it was as if she was not there, just a shadow, a whisper of a person drifting alongside the others. A ghost who neither laughed or smiled, cried or shied. She looked neither back nor forwards, always with her eyes lowered. They too were a shield, as if nothing could enter if she could not see it.

The two younger men — Jampa and Sonam — could have bounded away in front, taking days off their journey, but they did not. They shared the task of carrying Deyki with happy hearts, making fun where they could, eyes everywhere. They understood the dangers.

Tashi looked back. His homeland was passing through time to a place he would never be able to reach again. The trees now too small to see, the sparkling lakes now beyond the hills. He felt his spirit dying. It was like nothing he had felt in the hidden depths of his prison cell. A bereavement like no other, a physical pain in his heart, the pressing of grief at the back of his eyes. He felt a sob rise in his throat. He wanted to wail to the sky the long, drawn-out cry of an animal who had lost its mate. The love he felt for his country was the love of a spiritual culture as attached to the sacredness of the lakes and mountains as the gentle concept of Buddhism. And that attachment was real, tangible; and the tear he felt was as if his body was splitting in two. He mourned with all his being. Every cell in his body wept in silent pain.

He turned reluctantly to face the mountains, that great wall of separation which was the difference between life and death. He did not mind what he was crossing to, but he grieved with all his heart what he was crossing from. The land, the water, the sky of Tibet was also the land, the water and the sky in his bones. It was his DNA, He was born of these things, made of these things. The atoms in his body were composed of these things. They were inseparable, yet separate they must. It was a terrible wound which he must try and survive. For half of him would always remain in Tibet. The other half must survive as best it could. Maybe the old monk knew of these things and that is why he gave Tashi the manuscripts. To give a burden, to relieve a burden, that is the Tibetan way.

The climb turned into a scramble. The air crispened. The shaley rock gave way under their feet. For every inch gained, half an inch was lost. Their breathing laboured hard, but they pushed on, fear of being seen driving them. Jetsun, who was probably about fifty years old, found it most difficult, but never would she complain.

Steeper still was the climb. A faint path became visible as they twisted between the jagged grey boulders and the fledgling subnivean plants and shrubs on the sensitive area just below the snowline. The warming brought about by climate change was increasing the range of these shrubby plants and grasses. It was softening the snow too, but mostly it was the uncertainty of the weather that worried the guiding monk. Once they could have been sure of the seasons and generations of monk guides before him would have known exactly the right time to travel these foreboding peaks. Now, it was more a matter of luck. He hoped theirs would be of the good variety, and prayed accordingly, all the time keeping his thoughts to himself. He had been named Karma for good reason. His birth had brought his family joy and good health — or so they believed — thus his name was to reflect his life and, in time, it did. Joining a monastery was the most natural of outcomes, but becoming a guide had not been without its tribulations. His good actions did not necessarily bring about good outcomes for all in his care. He meditated upon this often, seeking a solution for the paradox.

The nun saw it first, amongst the lichen in the boulder-strewn depression they were walking. She ran up to it, caressing the soft violet flowers of many petals with her thin fingers. Pleased as they all were to find such beauty here amongst the rocky grey, they stood back for a moment. It was the first time she had shown any emotion towards anything at all.

She looked up towards them and spoke for the first time. "We call it Violet Care," and tears ran down her tiny face, and she buried her head in the little mass of flowers and sobbed. Karma walked gently up to her and squatted close beside her.

"Maybe it is a good sign to find such a thing on our journey."

She shook her head. "Maybe, but mostly it is a sign that the world is changing faster than our lives. I do not think it is changing well."

And she relapsed back into her careful silence, and moved away so that others could come close to the beautiful flower, and feel what they must, for the blue spectral light which brings violet to our eyes is vivid, and only just within the human range of vision. Such an important colour, one of the oldest colours used by humans. The colour of royalty and learning, humility and individualism, it has always evoked importance of one kind or another. But here on the northern windswept slopes of the Himalayas, it meant life, and light, and love. Life, because so little was expected to grow here, light, because of the brightness of the colour, and love, because of the feelings of warmth and care such a lonely little flower evoked.

They struck camp close to the flower, huddled close in their skins and blankets for warmth, a rug over their faces, and for some over their whole heads, for any warmth had to be conserved. But Karma and Tashi stared at the pinpricks of light beginning to show themselves overhead. The voyage of stars overhead they must come to know well, even if the night was cloudy, for the stars were their guide.

It was clear that night. There was no moon, and dusk was turning into night. As they lay on their backs, looking up, a wonderous sight gradually revealed itself to them. Peeping through the darkening skies were first a few little lights. Then a few more, then clusters of stars, then the incredible sight as the beautiful Milky Way wheeled slowly into view above the silhouetted mountain peaks. A million, million stars or more, clustered and exploding, white light and yellow light, unrepeatable patterns of nebula and dwarf stars, dots of light twenty-seven thousand light years away and a hundred and twenty light years wide. A conglomeration of gas and dust, the same atoms which make up every living thing, everywhere. From the purple flower to the mountain lion and the smallest fish in the sea, the clouds of potential life up there in the skies expanded and contracted, just waiting for the right combination to create yet more living things, somewhere, out there, just beyond our reach.

Meteors rushed by, man-made satellites, comets and shooting stars. The sky was alive. Tashi felt his core being lifted out of his chest to greet it. Intrinsically he wanted to be part of it, to join it. The feeling of euphoria took his breath away. He had lived in the mountains, but he had never seen this, or felt this, or wanted to be so much part of this.

Karma pointed his outstretched finger to the sky. He showed Tashi how to find the traveller's friend, the North Star, by locating the Big Dipper, shaped like a saucepan or plough, which always rotated anti-clockwise around the bright unwavering dot of light sitting directly above the North Pole. He pointed to the constellation of Cassiopeia on the opposite side of the North Star to the Big Dipper, and Orion with his three bright lights around his waist, the only three bright stars forming a short straight line in the entire sky. Easy to spot, and Tashi was delighted at how he could follow the shapes. Orion's belt was the name of the three stars in a line and, in this way, travellers could tell the direction of east and west all over the world. It was a magical experience, and a useful one, but he would need Karma to give the lesson more than once to properly be able to find the direction he needed.

"Just find the North Star, then look to the west. We are heading south-west, but not directly because the mountains sometimes make their own trails. It is a question of pragmatism. At times we might be heading east, or a little bit north, but as long as we keep the sky paths in our mind, we will not stray too far."

Tashi wanted to wake the others, to share the grandiose beauty unfolding above them, but Karma counselled against. They needed to rest. In the weeks ahead there would probably be other opportunities for them to see it and nothing would replace a good sleep, especially as from now on they would travel by night and sleep in the brightness of day.

Karma instructed that the next two days would mean walking later into the night and sleeping more by day. In this way, they could gradually shift their sleeping patterns until they slept all day and walked all night. He did not like to explain just how vital for their survival this would be, for Chinese army patrols combed these mountains for escapees and in these remote locations their fate would be entirely at the whim of the commanding officer.

And so, their fireside stories of sunset gradually became the fireside stories of dawn. Tibetans are well versed in the gift of storytelling. It is a sturdy tradition. Some stories were funny and filled the tight-packed circle of travellers with mirth. Some were philosophical, provoking conversation and debate. Others were sad and reinforced why they were undertaking such a risky journey. They bonded. The oldest and youngest quickly dozing away to sleep, the young men in hushed whispers planning what they would do when they reached freedom. Tashi dreamed of meeting the Dalai Lama, his spiritual leader, for whom he had suffered so much pain, for whom he would gladly lay down his life. If ever there was a god in human form, the Dalai Lama was this to Tashi. He dreamed of getting to North India where the Tibetan Government-in-Exile provided a core spiritual and cultural mainstay for Tibetan Buddhists everywhere. He dreamed of a place where monks could walk the streets in open conversation, where monks could travel the world in peace. He dreamed of harmony, of freedom of expression, of meeting those who had gone before him, of warmth and enough food, and maybe, just maybe, there would be a doctor who could heal his body. It was not his most important thought, for he expected to only live a short life. Yes, his most important, most golden, thought was to see the Dalai Lama, even for a second.

Clothing was checked, and their hands and feet were bound with rags to cover the gaps at the wrists and ankles to keep what warmth their bodies could muster through exercise close to the skin. It could be fatal to expose the skin to the extreme coldness they were expecting on the highest part of the route. No specialist clothing here, no mountain boots or soft down jackets for them. No lightweight fleece jackets or soft-shell pants. The clothes they wore were largely heavy layers given by well-wishers. They did not always fit well, they were often home-made, but they were of good natural materials, such as wool and the downy fur from the semi-wild yak who graze the lower slopes freely, and were as warm as any modern fibre.

For Tashi, it was the last chance to change his clothes. All embarrassment at his incontinence was forgotten. From now on he would have to walk in whatever human excrement he could not catch in a rag and he knew he did not have enough rags for the days ahead. Inevitably it would be a horrible journey, but he set his heart on the destination and freedom from fear and repression. He drank little, to minimise the urine he would inevitably pass without control, but moisture was the enemy. It would quickly freeze, paving the way for hypothermia and, in these frigid places, death.

For little Deyki, the clothes were cumbersome and heavy and so she was all trussed up like a chicken in her coat and hats and gloves and bindings. As the snow deepened, it was necessary to carry her most of the time and this they all shared with gusto and playful happiness, the young people tossing her from one to the other until she giggled herself silly. In the harshness of the mountains, on a restricted diet, and sleeping in crevices, they had happy days.

Now above the snowline, their dark shapes were invariably visible against the bright white of snow. It was not always possible to find a dark rocky outcrop or cliff to walk beside, so the risk of being seen had to be taken. At times they trudged through the soft downy powder of fresh fall, then at other times, it would be hard and icy. The glaciers were the most dangerous. Their surface had melted and frozen many times. They had shifted and creaked and fissured over centuries, and the danger of falling, or twisting a leg, was forever present. They went carefully and sometimes too slowly. Some small glaciers took all night to cross. They shimmered and glistened in wonderous shapes, and the rising moon created treacherous shadows, hiding the pocket traps and gaps. It was always with exhausted relief that the little party of rough-shod travellers reached the relative safety of firm rocky slopes.

One moonlit night, they were in a high mountain valley, traversing a sheet of deep snow in rhythmic single file. Heads bowed, determination in their faces. Plod. Plod. Plod. They were silent, concentrating only on the task in hand — to get through this place of high exposure as fast as possible. The moon was almost full, a gleaming headlamp in the sky, illuminating the snowscape as if it was day. They had a heightened sense of fear, for there was no meaningful cover within a mile or so either side of them, and the bright silvery light cast on them by the nearest celestial body to planet earth was reflected and magnified by the whiteness of the newly fallen snow. They took it in turns to lead, the hardest job of all being the breaking of a new pathway through the plateau. Youth and strength were needed to strike the first imprints in the yielding snow.

Towards the end of the night, Karma took the lead. He was followed by the cheerfully determined Tashi, Tenzin, then the nun, then Jetsun, Jampa and Sonam. Dekyi was having a short turn at walking to increase her body heat and was bringing up the rear because the snow was worn flatter by the footsteps of those in front. She was quite far behind, but they would wait for her to catch up every so often. There was no fear of losing each other on a clear night such as this.

A single shot rang out. It echoed sharply round the mountains. Karma's knees gave way under him and he crumpled to the ground. Tashi was labouring the few deep steps of snow up to him when another shot ran out.

The little figure at the back of the line dropped lifelessly into the snow.

They heard the gathering rumble of a distant avalanche. All was confusion and disbelief. With the echoes rebounding across the rocky walls, they did not even know where the shots were coming from. Instinctively they dropped to the ground, sinking themselves as far as they could into the snow and crawled to their wounded friends.

Tashi threw himself on Karma to protect him from further gunfire. "OK, OK," he gasped in panic. "You OK, my brother." And he cradled the young monk roughly in his arms.

Karma's eyes flickered and he smiled. "Very good that you learned the stars." And his body relaxed.

Tashi stuttered back in desperation, "I cannot do it. I cannot steer by the stars. I only have one eye."

"But it is a very good eye." And the last whispered words of the young guide hung steadily in the air.

Tashi shook him a little. "OK, my friend. You rest. I help you." And he frantically whispered the powerful healing mantra over and over again, "Om mani padme hum. Om mani padme hum," straining to let the sound sequence enter the innermost being of Karma, invoking the six realms of existence, calling on purity of mind and body, the indivisible union of wisdom, compassion and love.

Tears ran down the older monk's face as he rushed through the mantra over and over again. He was the one who was supposed to die, not this lively young monk who had not even begun to explore his sacred gifts. The tears froze almost before they left his eyes. He thought frantically of what could be done, how he could save this young and generous life, yet he did not even know where the bullet had entered Karma's body. There wasn't any blood, but the breathing, gentle, then faint, then nothing.

Tashi laid Karma's head gently in his lap. He had seen death before. Unjust, awful, painful death. The death that comes as a beautiful release. The death which comes slowly, and the death which comes suddenly. But this was a different death. This was an execution carried out from miles away by a person who would never see the bloom of youth on Karma's face, hear his voice, understand his smile. Death by something Tashi would never understand. A killing motivated by sport alone.

Tashi closed his eyes and whispered the first syllables of the Dying Prayer into the young monk's ear, rocking his body gently.

"Through the power of light which streams from you... may a good and peaceful death... benefit all other beings living or dead..."

And he looked up to the sky in beseeching question. There was only 'why'. There would only ever be 'why'. Why so much pain and hardship for gentle people? Why were they tortured, maimed and killed? Why was Buddhism so reviled? Why must people with weapons use them on the innocent? The answers would always evade him.

Tearing himself away from the oft-recited words, overcome with grief, unconscious that there had been a second shot, Tashi looked back along the thin line of travellers. Some were lying half-buried in the snow, but an even stronger sense of grief bore down on him as he grasped the meaning of the little scene behind him.

Just a few feet away lay the lifeless body of Deyki. Like a sleeping baby wrapped tight in a papoose, Jetsun had swaddled and cradled her little body, cooing soothing words over the child's open face, even as the blood seeped from her head into the snow, staining it red with the mark of a great injustice.

The little girl was already dead. Tashi howled to the sky. An animal cry of primeval origin. The others wept. Only the nun remained quiet, motionless, still suppressing the trauma which had never found a voice.

It was as if there was no point going on. Their guide was dead, their little charge too, violated, taken, executed for nothing but amusement. Just five years old. Tashi knew the minds of such people without understanding and the brown boots came into his mind's view. General Li Enlai.

Chapter 11
Reality Check

The return journey seemed determined to frustrate Firenza. First, there was security. Firenza was the type of woman who tended to wear a lot of metal. In her ears, on her fingers, round her neck, round her waist. She had weighed up the cost of wearing her usual clunky jewellery and debated with herself the cost of not wearing it. In the event, she met herself halfway and wore some of it.

There had been security issues on international flights in the past few years. People attempting to smuggle through the ingredients of bomb-making kits piecemeal seemed to draw the most attention. A group of young people had almost succeeded in blowing up a passenger plane. They had, between them, carried small amounts of ammonium nitrate, aluminium, a travel clock, nail varnish remover and some tools. Carefully they had passed the materials from one to another and, carried in one small bag, one of them went into the toilet to put it all together. Fortunately for everyone else on the plane, he only succeeded in burning himself, but the authorities used the event to clamp down heavily on all passengers at all times. Unknown to the general public, many governments were constantly in a high state of alarm. It had never been clarified who the bomb-making group were, or who they were working for, or indeed what their motive was. They seemed to have been spirited away. Notionally democratic governments were becoming increasingly worried about their lack of popularity and misguided forays into other countries had plunged the ratings of many into spiralling depths of public disapproval. Millions were dying of hunger and war. World tensions were climbing higher every day and a general realignment of political allies was taking place. A successful aeroplane explosion, in the right place, whether a false flag operation or not, could upset the lines of uneasy truce between the oil-producing nations and those determined to work with renewable energy.

The world was becoming more dangerous and polarised and, apart from the usual bombing attempts shouted loud on the news, Firenza was largely in ignorance of what was unfolding around her.

Trying not to be conscious of the tiny memory card stitched in her bra, she dutifully took off her belt, her shoes, her scarf, her bracelets and the keys in her pocket. The scanner beeped insistently as she went under it. The security staff motioned that she should go back and try again, but without the rings. She did and still the scanner was still not happy. Eventually, she removed her earrings and her watch and the scanner seemed satisfied. A quick pat-down revealed nothing of interest and she retrieved her previous ornaments, taking an inordinate time to put them all back on and holding up a queue of mildly disgruntled fellow travellers.

The palaver through security had been enough. Under normal circumstances, such a fuss would have flustered her, but today it served her well. Someone with something to hide would not have drawn such attention to herself.

Upon landing at Heathrow airport, she retrieved her rucksack, and immediately knew it had been opened. Of course, it was the right of the authorities to open it, but it felt uncomfortable just the same. She shuddered slightly. Putting the photographs of the burning monk into the right hands was a high priority.

They had landed late at night. She and Margot had briefly discussed which papers they would each approach. Margot had contacts with some of the fringe online publications and Firenza thought she could find some mainstream journalists through work. She, in fact, already knew a few, but they were tied to the advertising wing of the organisations and not the news/politics people who would be most appropriate. But she thought it best to start with someone she knew and work from there.

The next morning Firenza breezed into work as usual. She had agonised herself almost to death during the night over what to wear on her first day back and who she should approach first, second, third, in her quest to get the pictures and the note published.

Although young in years, she was sceptical in the extreme of going to any government department or charitable organisation. She knew well enough they could not be trusted to do anything useful with the information. Everything was corrupt from the prime minister down. She ran through a few scenarios in her mind, all of which were make-believe and ended with her being either heroic or devastated. Nothing came even close to reality. In the event, she lost a lot of sleep and plumped for the red high heels, matching handbag and a simple black dress adorned with her grandmother's brooch for luck. It wasn't a lucky brooch, but if she had a good day, it would become her lucky brooch.

The task weighed more heavily on her than she imagined, though she was extra careful to appear her bright engaging self. She was distracted during her work update and found it unusually difficult to concentrate. At the first coffee break (you could take as many as you liked in Beaufort Advertising), she made a bee line for a person with whom she was vaguely acquainted in the department which liaised with external press.

"Hi, Andy!" she breezed nonchalantly as she came to a halt in front of his desk.

He looked up, a question mark on his face. He did not know she had been away, in fact, he barely recognised her.

"Ah," he said, in having scoured his brain for a sign of recognition. "Your hair was green last time I saw you."

She had momentarily forgotten what colour her hair was at that actual moment and a hand went up to inspect it, as if by feeling it she could tell the colour.

"Yea, it's the washed-out purple look at the moment. I've been travelling."

"So, what brings you to external publications?" He was still floundering for her name and hoped he'd stumble upon it before the conversation became embarrassing.

Firenza wasn't the indirect type. Being indirect always irritated her. Her mother was indirect in almost everything. Her mother would talk all around the houses to get to the subject she sought and even then, you had to guess at what she wanted. If her mother wanted to go out to lunch, she would first ask what time it was, then discuss what time she had breakfast, then table the restaurants or cafés which were likely to be closed, then recount the various experiences friends might have had in eateries which might be open, then run through imaginary menus until Firenza was tearing out her hair. She put it down to her mother being born under the sign of Cancer, thus the crab-like, indirect approach. Firenza was a Leo. Terrifyingly direct. She launched straight to the point.

"Do you happen to know any journalists in the news or politics sections of any of the papers we deal with?"

Andy raised a surprised eyebrow. He was very proud of this muscular achievement and relished any opportunity to use it.

Having suitably impressed this young woman with his eyebrow performance, he sat back in his chair to give the matter due thought.

"Well, I don't have direct dealings with them, but now and then I meet up for a drink in the pub where lots of journalists gather. The Rose and Crown, down on the river, do you know it?"

She did, but it wasn't leading her to the thing she wanted. A name and a telephone number would be a good start.

"Do you have the number of an individual I could contact? I have a bit of an interesting news story." She wasn't sure whether to go full on with the story or stay vague. It seemed more sensible to start vague; she could always be pressed for more details later if required. In any case, it could hardly be a hot scoop if she told anyone about it. Confidentiality even, or especially if asked for, was almost impossible in the hothouse office environment in which they worked. Any gossip was good gossip. Her story, she knew, was far from gossip, but the ramifications of unfolding even a little piece of the story could backfire. People would be delighted to think it affected her mental health, her ability to do the job, her inability to hold on to her boyfriend, the colour of her eyeliner... you name it, the office piranhas would be in a feeding frenzy behind her back.

"Ah, how enigmatic." Andy seemed proud of his use of language and lingered on the word 'enigmatic' for a few seconds. "Do you want to tell me more? I know one or two people, but knowing the subject would help."

His eyes alighted on her short skirt and high heels (it didn't matter to him what colour they were) and noted her long legs. A bit skinny for his tastes, but shaped nicely.

Firenza smiled sweetly. This man might be her only chance to avoid cold-calling every journalist in town. She would play the game and lowered her eyes in what she hoped was quaint embarrassment, forgiving herself for the momentary abandonment of hard-won feminism. "Well, I'd rather not say right now. It's a bit confidential." She stopped herself saying that 'she was only asking for a friend', though the hackneyed idea did briefly cross her mind.

"Could you introduce me to someone? Maybe by email?" She stayed casual, as if it didn't matter too much either way, but was conscious that time was getting away from her and her empty chair would soon be noticed.

Andy then entered his time-honoured flirtation mode, in which he assumed the character of a raven-haired Lothario, completely at odds with the incontrovertible fact that he was balding and had a squint. The silly game was amusing and irritating at the same time. "I could probably do that, maybe over lunch one day." He studied his diary in a sickeningly supercilious way, as if she had already accepted the invitation.

"That would be lovely," she replied, hoping a little white lie for a good cause might be forgiven. "But the matter is a bit urgent, and I'd like to talk to somebody today really. It's quite all right if you can't help," and her eyes scanned the room for someone who possibly could.

Andy Bream felt his chances of impressing this young woman, and indeed the entire open-plan office of some forty-seven people, were ebbing quickly away.

"Just give me a minute." He racked his brains and, simultaneously, his online address book for someone impressive to put her in touch with. Not too impressive, but impressive enough for a twenty-three-year-old girl with scant experience of the real world, which importantly would put him a notch or two up in her estimation.

The name Isaac Brierly came into view. He knew Isaac fairly well. Isaac was a bit older than himself, but knew almost everybody in the press world, so would at least be a good start for the young woman standing in front of him, who was already shifting her weight from one stilettoed heel to the other in barely disguised impatience. Isaac would at least be happy that a pretty young woman had been put in touch with him and it was just possible that he would be able to steer Firenza in the right direction, so it looked like brownie points all around from Andy's point of view.

Andy Bream wrote the name and two numbers on the back of his ostentatiously monogrammed business card.

"Isaac Brierly is a good bloke, knows a lot of people. Try him, and don't forget to mention my name."

She took the card quickly and examined it. She checked she could read the mobile numbers — one for work, one for... who knew.

"So, when do we have that lunch, you promised me?"

She had promised him no such thing. But she might, in fact, owe him lunch if this contact worked out, but absolutely nothing more. "Ring me next week when I'm properly settled in." And she breezed away with a wave.

An hour later Firenza was on the phone to Isaac Brierly, quietly, on her personal mobile, in a storage cupboard on the next floor down.

"Hello, is that Isaac Brierly?" She started with the obvious niceties, tense and a bit frightened, trying to gauge the tone of his voice, his mood.

"Y e s," he drawled, spinning the word out to its utmost. She detected a slight American accent and pictured him with his feet up on a paper-strewn desk, lying back on a recliner chair.

She relaxed a bit. "Andy Bream kindly gave me your number this morning. I have some photographic evidence for a story you might be interested in." This much she had rehearsed at home in the dark hours of non-sleep.

Andy Bream had, in fact, already rung Isaac on a third number — the private number which was used for all manner of non-family, non-work issues. The really private number. Andy had mentioned the high heels and a few other things besides.

"I s e e," came the lazily constructed reply.

"It's rather urgent and I'd rather not discuss it on the phone network. Can we meet in an hour or so?"

Isaac was a fairly senior manager at the Sertus News Agency. He didn't have a great deal to do that afternoon. His staff did all the slogging work of news gathering. He wouldn't be needed in an executive capacity until later in the day and he was bored with the humdrum of the daily grind. Only now and again did anything happen which interested him. The rest was a never-ending churn of pointless presidential debates and even more pointless wars. In truth, there was still a shred of morality in him, despite the years of being a hack, and he would rather be counting the bodies of presidents than the people they purported to represent, so an hour or so out of the office was a timely invitation. He didn't suppose that whatever story this young person thought she had would be particularly interesting, but a young fresh face might help the day along.

He sounded a bit more interested. "I can meet you at Café Roma in an hour or so."

Firenza knew then that Andy must already have spoken to him. Quite obviously Isaac knew where she worked. It was a bit annoying, but what could she do. "Yes, OK see you there at about 1.30."

She automatically slipped out of her high heels into the usual battered rubber boots. The rain wasn't too bad today, but it was incessant. It had been for years, with just a few breaks. Too few. This was Britain and nobody talked about the weather any more. Perhaps they didn't want to encourage it.

The shabby little café was friendly enough, the floor wet and showing signs of muddiness after the morning's customers. As it was only drizzling, Firenza suggested they sit outside under the large prefabricated canvas covers.

She eyed him up. He was not as corpulent as his telephone manner suggested, but pleasantly middle-aged with a flair of wavy grey hair streaked with black. His clothes were subtle and the quality looked good. Firenza wondered if she could trust him.

"I can't use it," he said bluntly when she told him what she had. "It's awful, it's wrong, it's tragic, I know, but this sort of thing only puts China in a bad light. The new alignment of world powers since the US subsumed the south of the continent has put the British government firmly in the camp of the Chinese. We are ramping up trade, cutting import taxes, and shaping up exchange universities. This kind of story, if published, would undo years of diplomatic work. We can't use it."

"What about the general, Li Enlai? Can't you do something about him?"

Firenza was trying to decide how to feel. Moral outrage was on a slow burn in her chest. She had barely passed the simplistic stage of thinking what was right was right, and what was wrong, wrong.

"I can promise to do no more than think about that one. The situation in Tibet is contentious and all news agencies of any note are instructed to downplay any issues arising there. We do not have a free hand any more. If I published your photographs, Sertus would be closed down. In any case, this is not the first time a monk in Tibet has protested in this way, and it's probably not going to be the last."

"But the general. We have his name. We have the note. Look, I have it here on my phone."

She scrolled quickly through the pictures on her memory card and showed him the crudely written scrap of dog-eared paper.

I Dorjee Wangdu
I monk at Labrang Monastery
Chinese want destroy Tibetan life Destroy monastery Destroy monks.
Very much torture. Very much sadness
Please tell world General Li Enlai very bad man. Kill many nuns and monks.

I give life you stop him. Life for Free Tibet

Isaac Brierly finished his coffee and sat back in the small rattan chair. "It's all true," he said. "Terrible things are happening out there. Terrible things are happening everywhere and there is very little you and I can do about it."

"But that doesn't mean we shouldn't try and do something."

He shook his head sadly.

"Is it so very hard to right a wrong?"

"You can always try on your own, but if you get too close to success someone will stop you, or you will just 'disappear' along with most of the other human rights defenders," and he opened his hands into the air as if he was disappearing someone with the utmost ease.

Firenza was incredulous. She knew corruption was a way of life, so too was suppression, but with this incontrovertible proof in her hands, she felt it could be possible to punch through it.

Isaac read her face. "I'm truly, deeply sorry. If your pictures are of good enough quality, you might find one of the fringe websites to publish. They pop up all the time."

Yes, thought Firenza, and they are closed down all the time.

She left the café in deep despair. It was not so much that she was politically naïve, which she inevitably was as the result of a quiet upbringing in the rural lands, but that she felt powerless to help someone in need. The scene of the immolation went slowly through her mind again.

Back at her desk, a slow depression was settling around her. She tried her bright smile when people spoke to her, but it was false. She simply did not know enough about the world to know what to do next. Her next meeting with Margot was a long week away. In the meantime, she would apply herself to an information-gathering exercise, quietly, at home.

A person she did not know put an envelope on her desk. She wasn't in the mood for Andy Bream's pretentious lunch invitation and pushed it to one side.

Chapter 12
The Trial Begins

The dead were buried in the snow and their meagre rations duly taken. Tashi and the young men took it in turns to lead the despondent, and so tragically depleted, travellers. The skies were clear. They suspected they were being followed. Cat and mouse and the mouse had nowhere to hide.

The open plateau of soft snow seemed to go on forever. Each knew they were a target. They tried to walk two abreast to shield each other, but the going was too hard. Tremulously they forged on in single file, in silence, listening for something, they knew not what, which might warn them to drop into the snow for cover.

The night wore carefully into a cloudy morning. There was no sun to convey them the slightest warmth and the wind rose. It came from every direction, twirling and unfurling its icy tendrils around each defenceless human being, adding to their sense of exhaustion and helplessness. It gnawed at their faces, their raggy clothes. It sucked away from their bodies what little heat they could manufacture, and it drove them away from each other as they stoically tried to stay in line to minimise the effort of breaking new snow. More than once, someone lost their step and fell. Every time the person behind would rush as quickly as they could to pick them up. This was no place for rest and fear drove them on.

It was mid-morning before they reached the cover of some boulders which had freshly detached themselves from a larger mass of rock. They slumped gratefully, arms around each other in crumpled fright and sorrow. They could not eat, but exhaustion forced a fitful and stiffening sleep. All except the little nun, who stayed awake, alert, stiff-backed, still as ice.

Just a few hours, some had less, but it was enough to help them carry themselves forward into the next night of struggle. They ate a little and shouldered their bags ready for the uncertain climb ahead. Tashi was uncertain about more than the climb, for the clouds now obscured the stars, and his rudimentary lessons in star navigation were about to be useless. He scanned the sky often, looking for a break in the cloud which might reveal something familiar, but it was not to be, this night. This first night of lonely, despairing climb, hand over foot, in the darkness of night, where the rocks gave way under your hands and feet, when you lost your sense of direction, when nothing was possible except the grunt of exertion, and the occasional whisper to check everybody was still close by.

Fingers found crevices. Feet found ledges, sometimes, but not every time. Dislodged stones, sharp and loose, fell onto those labouring below and on they went, unsure how far, not knowing if it was the best route, blinded by night and low cloud and searing wind.

The late morning light came before they had completed the climb. They were tucked into the mountains, shielded on all sides by rock, jagged and treacherous. They started to chat, buoying each other up, trying to revive spirits and energy. Nobody spoke of the night before. Jampa, who was a natural climber, spotted a ledge to the side of them and they inched their way across the rock face onto it and, wrapped onto each other with whatever came to hand, and once again collapsed in untidy and insecure rest.

Jetsun was the last to make the ledge. She was strong in mind and robust in health, but she was not young. The climb, though not particularly sheer, was as much as she could manage. They were not getting enough rest, Tashi could see that. He did not wish to be their leader, or a decision-maker of any kind, but he knew that they would have to find somewhere sheltered to rest very soon before they started giving way to despondency and fatigue.

Jampa read his mind. "The climb is too difficult for them. I will go ahead and find somewhere we can make camp for maybe two days."

Tashi nodded, glad that Jampa had found the courage to volunteer. "Yes, everyone must rest." He fumbled in his inner pocket for the compass which he had taken from Karma's lifeless body. "Here, take this, my friend. It will help you find your way back to us."

"I cannot." Jampa pressed the little instrument back into Tashi's hand. "If I do not come back, it will be lost and you will need it if the skies are cloudy."

They sat in thoughtful silence, cross-legged, foreheads close together, thinking through the many scenarios ahead. There was no guarantee they would make it through the next hour, never mind the next day.

After a long reflection, Tashi said, "Here are our choices. We stay together and hope to find somewhere safe in a few hours. Or you go ahead and find a good place — but might have an accident, or fall, or not be able to find us again. Or maybe you don't find a good place and we have to go on blindly, and your sacrifice is wasted."

Jampa hummed thoughtfully and looked at the retched little band of exiles. "I only know that they are so tired."

"We cannot stay here, it is too dangerous and too open to the wind, and we will freeze. Let us go on together for a few hours and review the position then."

It was now mid-morning and still the skies were dark and ominous. The tops of the mountains were shrouded, out of sight, but not out of mind. They talked through the options and decided to work their way round the side of the cliff in the hope of getting a view of the upcoming landscape.

Wearily, oh so wearily, they picked up their bags and with a reluctance to move born as much by sadness and plunging morale, as by fatigue, they stretched their tired bones and muscles, ate a sparse meal of salted meat and flatbread, and once again inched round the brown-bouldered mountain. Tashi calculated they had been travelling for ten or twelve nights, which maybe meant they were in sight of the halfway mark of their journey. When he was sure of where they were on the route, he would tell them the good news. They were all probably counting the days and nights for themselves and no doubt each would come to different conclusions, as switching from day trekking to night trekking and back again confused the mind. He guessed they would run out of food before they got to the Nepali border and the stories he had heard about little villages tucked away in the Himalayas, were alternatively hopeful and impossible. It was only hope that they had. He would work with that.

Edging round the difficult climb, everything suddenly changed. In front was an incredible view of the far mountains, now not so far. The clouds cleared and though most of the lower peaks were in dusky darkness in the late afternoon sun, one stood out. A pinnacle of rosy-gold rock threw itself to the sky as if to be sure of its place as the highest mountain in the world. It was glinting, jagged, like a huge uncut jewel demanding defiance of the elements. High in the sub-tropical jet stream, the purple hues of orographic uplift whisked vortices southwards on the freezing wind like a flag pointing the way to a new life.

Everyone clumped together to look. They were a very long way from home, but they knew this sight meant they were heading in the right direction at least, and where the huge bulky shape of Everest, the Goddess Mother of Mountains, the Chomolungama of legend, the respected, the sacred and beloved spirit of all high places, stood tall and firm, travellers could feel a tangible connection with the natural world and connect more readily with the rich vein of Buddhist intellectual practice which had for generations revered this place. They moved gingerly past the steepest part of the rock face and found impromptu places to kneel before this great symbol of strength and spiritual wealth and, as they looked, the sun gradually sank, turning the beautiful layers of strata on the north face of the mountain from gold, to rose, to mauve and finally to darkness. They opened their hearts and prayed and felt spiritually refreshed.

Jampa, too, had fallen to his knees in reverence, but prayer for him would take second place to survival. His eyes had been quick to map out a gentle path leading down to the elevated valley floor spreading out below.

He stirred his comrades. "We must be quick before the light fades, for it is blackness itself in these grumbling rocks. Follow me."

They filed downwards after him, more hopeful than they had been for many days. Tashi, too, had tried to map out the land, but he was not a natural mountain man and was entirely content to follow the advice of his younger friend. The stars poked between the thinning cloud that night and the moon wavered on its reductive course from the bright and compromising full to the waxing gibbous bulge which signalled the descent to the safer luminosity of a crescent. If everything worked to plan, they should reach the border before the next new moon.

The route Jampa chose was not strictly in the direction they needed, but more than direction, right now they needed an easy way down the mountain and a flat, sheltered place to rest.

The moon, now a kinder friend, helped. They became less anxious about the people with guns who might have been following them. It was quite possible that the cliff they had scaled enabled a natural buffer from the threat. In any case, it did no good to worry about the things over which they had no control. Worry weakened a person, a glad heart strengthened.

They struck camp, lamenting that there was no means on these higher slopes to light a fire. They spread out. They slept alongside each other, like felled logs in a quiet pond, relaxed at last.

Chapter 13
The Beginning

She tidied her desk as usual when it was time to go home and forced herself to open the plain white envelope. Such an old-fashioned touch in a world where everything happened electronically and instantly, whether you liked it or not.

It was not from Andy Bream.

In large loose letters was written:

I may be able to help. Call me on this number. O01 518 675 1953
Isaac

Clearly, Isaac had omitted to say precisely what form that help might take, but it was a glimmer of hope and hope was all she had.

Once home, she made herself a sandwich of whatever was not covered in mould, slumped heavily into her one comfortable armchair, second-hand, a bit worn on the arms, and so heavy it took three people to woman-handle it up the stairs, and mused on her future.

She had a mortgage to pay. She had never particularly liked her job and today she felt that she had suddenly outgrown it. Being a junior advertising executive was just another way of saying she was a dogsbody with creative potential. Advertising was only really another form of manipulation, or maybe it was pure propaganda turned respectable. The nagging feeling that she was part of a machine which spent millions trying to sell a product or service to people who neither wanted nor needed it was never far from her mind. And if she was not going to be in advertising, she might not need to live in such an expensive part of the city. In fact, she might not need to live in a city at all. She disliked the smell of cities, the noise, the crowds, the dirt. She disliked the way the rain was always dirty and she had to wash her hair every day. She did not like the hypocrisy of having to wear waterproof boots every single day because of climate change, yet working for contracts with products and packaging and which actually made it all worse.

The things which she had put to the back of her mind because she was not sufficiently motivated to think about them carefully, were suddenly at the front of her mind. It wasn't so much the sacrifice of the burning monk which was making her think this way, as the horrible confirmation that his sacrifice was rendered pointless because Britain was making trade agreements with China.

It was only right, in her mind, that she try harder. She rang Isaac's number.

"Hi, I got your note."

"Firenza," he drawled, giving the seven-syllable word plenty of space to breathe.

"I have done a bit of digging about your general in the plumbing of the newsroom and I would appreciate your confidentiality on this matter, or we will both be in trouble."

Firenza was quite surprised that he had taken any trouble at all and indeed had taken such a risk. She had more or less expected that he would simply pass her on to someone else and that she would thereafter be fobbed round journalistic circles until the day she died.

Her fast, affirmative response reflected the eagerness of inexperience, or at least experience which had never had to keep a confidence of any importance.

"Firenza, this matter of the general is of feasible concern to human rights organisations. You have given us a name. People will be taking great risks to check its veracity."

Firenza chewed her bottom lip thoughtfully. "I may not understand the depth of what you are telling me, but I think I understand enough, and I can keep a confidence." She ruefully acknowledged to herself that the only type of confidence she had so far been required to keep revolved around a friend's clandestine activities with a certain young man she didn't even know. It had hardly been a state secret.

"O — K," Isaac assented in his normal relaxed style, quite at odds with the tension of the moment. "Here's what I need you to do. Put the photographs on a memory card and put that in an envelope. I'll give you the address another time." And the phone went dead.

Firenza surveyed her tiny flat. It amounted to one visibly worn armchair, a sagging sofa bed and a few kitchen utensils. There was more staircase than flat. It had seemed like the pinnacle of achievement in her life, yet suddenly it bothered her and she didn't want it.

Equally suddenly the thought of renting a small place in the country seemed like a good idea and she took a ride round the internet. It was easy to see that the further you got from the city, any city, the cheaper the rents were. Amazingly, she could rent an entire cottage in the centre of Wales for a minute fraction of what London costs were. It wasn't just escape she sought, it was time. More than anything she needed to step off the hamster wheel of pointless work and really think about the world and the place she would like within it.

She asked her homebot, Ravena, for some city news to distract her from inconclusive thoughts. It had been a while since the weather was news, but it appeared that tonight it had crept back up the agenda. A particularly deep depression was forming to the north of Scotland and progressing south-east towards Scandinavia. On its own, this would not be amazing news, but the storm surge was going to coincide with an exceptionally high tide and a lot of extra rainfall. The really big news was that the Thames Barrier might not cope with the level of water, and the unthinkable could happen — London would flood. The people on the radio were beside themselves with thinly disguised glee. They were delighted to have some actual news to report, instead of the veiled propaganda stuffed in their inboxes about wars no one was accountable for and politicians who took hypocrisy to new depths and still pretended to be on the side of the people.

It was depressing. Here she was in a job she didn't like, in a flat she could not afford in a city past its sell-by date. The way ahead suddenly became clear; sell the flat whilst the market was reasonably buoyant and get out of town.

She caught up with some friends on the social web and was about to turn in for bed when Ravena announced a call.

"Take this down quickly. Three Bentinick Mansions, London." And the connection ended. Firenza dashed headlong across the tiny room and fell over herself to find something to scribble with before she forgot the address.

Wow, she thought, nursing the new bruise from the table she clonked into, talk about clandestine.

It would remain to be seen if this had been clandestine enough.

The photographs had been copied already, but Firenza was unsure about going to a mansion building alone. If what she was doing was indeed risky, being trapped inside an unknown building didn't seem too clever.

She would wait and talk to Margot. It was all a bit awe-inspiring and dreadful at the same time.

As if on cue, Margot contacted her the next day and asked if they could meet up earlier than planned. Firenza did not have a great deal planned in the social sense, so they agreed to meet the next day at lunchtime if the rain wasn't too bad.

They met at one of the last of the old department stores in the last of the old shopping streets left in the last prestigious parts of the city. Nobody really wanted the things they had to sell any more, but people still liked to visit for old time's sake. The store was a little tired and worn, but it kept up appearances with pretty window displays and happy music. These stores were more of a shop window for online sales, but fewer and fewer people ventured out these days. The weather, the risk of infection, the pointlessness of browsing, the difficulties of travel, all conspired to bring the old world to a shabby, stuttering close.

Firenza went in through one of the sets of double doors leading straight off the street. A waft of fuggy cosmetic and perfume smells greeted her. Lipsticks, powder, face creams, they all had their weird fragrance. She smiled to herself. Blended together the air was full of the unmistakable smell of the bourgeoisie. A dying breed. Nobody had told them the party was over. Firenza wore makeup. She loved it. But hers was mashed together by friends, keen not to have anything tested on animals. The stuff in the store was all made by one company and sold under different names as if to imply more choice and competitive pricing. It was laughably overpriced so that all the marketing and expensive packaging could be paid for. She smiled ruefully — so that people like her could be paid for. But here Firenza did not see lipstick. She saw little animals in cages, suffering.

Upstairs there was a small coffee shop with exotic pastries under glass next to the toilets as was the time-honoured way.

"Don't let the buggers get you down," whispered Margot from behind, not that Margot could whisper.

Firenza turned, smiling. It was good to see Margot. She was wearing the most boring two-piece she had ever seen in the world. It was a pinky-brown non-colour and was buttoned tight across her ample bosom.

"Whatever are you wearing?" exclaimed Firenza in tactless exclamation.

"I've put on weight. Can't be helped." Margot boomed in her familiar decibel level, undid the complaining buttons on her jacket and brushed aside the conversation to order two coffees without stopping to ask what type of coffee Firenza would like.

It was all rather reassuring. Firenza had been feeling isolated with the secret, the story, the knowledge. Out of her depth with Isaac and his weird instructions, she was on the brink of wondering if she should entertain thoughts of paranoia.

They sat down and exchanged stories amid the banter and bubble of other people doing something similar. Firenza looked around the room eyeing everybody up to see who could be eves-dropping. She wondered if paranoia had already crept up on her.

"You're quiet," said Margot. "Where's your bright colours?"

"I haven't felt too colourful just lately."

"Yup," Margot beamed cheerfully. "Immolations and torture are not exactly festive business. But it would be good if you didn't make any drastic changes to your appearance for the time being. Ninety-nine per cent of communication is non-verbal, you know," and she rolled her eyes to the ceiling for effect.

Firenza wasn't in a jocular mood. She told Margot about her conversation with Isaac Brierly.

Margot visibly brightened, if that was possible. "Have you got time now? We could go together to that address right now if you like? There wasn't any time specified was there?"

"Yes. Good idea. Let's get it out of the way now," said Firenza. "I can be a bit late back to work, it won't matter much." Well, it wasn't going to matter at all if she was leaving the company.

They downed the coffee and went back out into the plopping rain. There were so many kinds of rain. This was the rain of large ploppy drops, not too many of them, but very wet just the same. In dull moments, Firenza amused herself by dreaming up names for all the different types of rain. There was the usual pouring, drizzle and mist, but her new insightful vocabulary now included plopping, mogging — which was something between mist and fog — misering — which is dreary and dirty — and spicking — which is sharp little spikes of cold rain. She had developed quite a list.

Plopping was turning to pouring by the time they had crossed the city to the street on which Bentinick Mansions stood. Number three was a huge brick mansion with an imposing entrance atop a flight of stone steps. The old oak doors sported bevelled glass and polished brass footplates, doorknobs, letter boxes, you name it. On either side of the doors, stone-carved coats-of-arms featuring a rampant lion and a griffin parading around an obscure heraldic symbol on the verge of being lost to time. Probably someone, somewhere, kept a record of these things, but the world had moved on, leaving the aristocracy cowering under the dilapidated roofs of their crumbling stately homes, once open to the public to garner enough money for the upkeep, but the public was no longer interested. Neither was the aristocracy.

Firenza and Margot marched boldly up the stairs and pressed the buzzer next to the ornate number 3.

"Who is calling?" came the disjointed and fuzzy voice.

"Me, Firenza Blackamore," said Firenza, "and my friend, Margot."

The door clicked quietly and they pushed it open. Inside it was exactly as could have been predicted from the outside; a massive oak staircase, suitably carved to the standards of high Victorian splendour. Dark wood panelling everywhere, polished wood floors, and the entire room smelling of a heady mix of lavender and beeswax. Above was the obligatory chandelier hanging straight through five or six floors, around which the staircase curved according to the gifted eye of the architect and the epic skill of the craftsmen who brought this wonderous piece of work through the birth canal of forest and chisel into the service of the wealthy family whose feet once pattered up and down these polished floors.

Firenza and Margot could only look with appreciation at their surroundings. Everything was worth studying, from the gargoyles on the wood-clad pillars, to the cut crystal droplets of the chandelier.

The sound of a light-footed person coming down the stairs drew their attention. He stopped before reaching the bottom and motioned that they follow him back up.

"Bill," he said, extending the back of his wrist in common greeting. Firenza and Margot did likewise.

Bill led them to the second floor and through an inevitable large oak door. On the other side, a pale girl sat staring at a screen. She turned to smile at them.

"Thank you for taking the risk to come and meet us," she said in a mild, slightly foreign voice. "Please sit down. Bill will get us some refreshments."

Firenza had not thought she was taking much of a risk to come here, especially since the capable Margot was with her.

They sat down at a flimsy kitchen table. The inside of this apartment was at extreme odds with the rest of the building. It looked as though it had been hurriedly flung together. Just a table, a couple of laptops and some old plastic chairs.

"My name is Lulu," said the girl, who was not, upon closer inspection a girl at all, just small, and slim, and quietly spoken. When she moved, the air around her stayed still. She moved like a benign spirit from a distant world. She might have been thirty-five. It was hard to tell under the huge glasses.

"Trust is a curious thing," she started, and Firenza noticed that she did not say her 'r's' clearly. The 'r' came out sounding a bit like a 'w', so trust sounded more like 'twust'.

"I do not know if I can trust you and you do not know if you can trust me, so maybe we have to take each other completely 'on trust'." She smiled slightly at her small joke.

"I am going to trust you, because you have seen what others have not seen and you have evidence to prove it. By all accounts, you have been moved by this episode and have earnestly attempted to bring it to public attention. Also, you have, I understand, a note passed to you from a monk."

Firenza looked at Margot. It would be better to just pass everything over and be done with the whole episode. Margot nodded assent.

"I guess we have to trust you right back or there will be no progress. I need a moment please." She turned with her back to the room, shuffling into her bra where the memory card was lodged.

"There." And she placed the minute storage device on the table, pushing it away with her finger as she recalled what was on it. The image of the burning monk impressed itself once more on the back of her retina. She knew it might take days to leave her.

"Thank you so much," said Lulu in gratitude, so disarming, and so quiet it was barely audible. "Now I have to trust you more."

Firenza shifted in her seat, she wasn't sure she like the sound of this.

"We are a human rights organisation. Not a mainstream one that you might have heard of. We are slightly undercover, information gathering mostly. Sometimes we hand our findings onto a public-facing outfit like Amnesty and sometimes we do not. We have to make decisions."

Bill came back with some green tea and sat down with them.

Lulu continued. "In the case of what I believe is on this card, we need to keep the contents to ourselves. You already know that no one will publish the pictures because the burgeoning British trading relationship with China will not be allowed to be put in jeopardy.

"Britain is a tiny country, overpopulated and unable to feed itself without imports. Mainland China is short of land and resources despite the complete moratorium on childbirth, but China owns most of the arable land in Africa and is in a strong trading position, especially as the US has turned inwards and has inevitably become toothless. The US is more interested in fighting itself than taking part in international treaties. The power of Europe is some protection for Britain, but not much. The situation is flimsy if Britain is to avoid a period of near starvation."

Margot was aware of the global picture, but Firenza was only dimly cognisant. She had not thought her country was on the brink of starvation, but, there again, she was in advertising and coming up with a cheerful ditty to sell a tin of rice was hardly an introduction to world affairs. There again, why was she selling rice in tins when rice did not grow in Britain? It was worth thinking about.

"Your note, I believe, mentions the name of Li Enlai. General Li has been in our sights for some years. By all accounts, he is a vile and ruthless man. We have reason to believe he is to be part of an exchange mission to Britain. The British army are outsourcing some of their training to China. The British government feels that, after a couple of decades of relative international peace, the fighting force of this country has, so to speak, gone soft. It is hoped that by exchanging training methods with our new ally, both sides will benefit. General Li, for no sensible reason we can think of — apart from the fact that they may want to get him out of Tibet to limit his notoriety — will be part of this delegation."

"What do you plan to do then?" asked Margot, who had been unusually quiet. "I mean, when he is in England? And where do we fit in?"

Lulu sighed. "Our first wish is to have him arrested, charged by the International Criminal Court and tried. This is why we have been collecting evidence."

"But our note is hardly a big bit of evidence," chipped in Firenza.

"Surprisingly, and together with the photographs, it is serious evidence. But there is something more we would ask of you."

Silence.

Lulu paused because she didn't know how to ask. The others just paused in expectation.

"Sounds a bit ominous," said Firenza finally, unpractised as to the art of silence. The others nodded faintly.

"We may need a safe house, that's all. We ask if you would agree for us to have access to yours. I believe it is the centre of the city?"

Firenza, always inclined to be helpful, tried to think through the implications. How dangerous was it for her personally? How many people would have to fit in? How would this work if she wanted to sell it? Who were these people anyway?

"I — um — am thinking of selling it actually," she ventured.

"We are thinking in the very short term," said Lulu. "Like in the next week or so. It's OK if you can't do it, and we may not actually need it anyway, it's just a way of allowing for contingencies."

It was probably unwise to ask what sort of contingencies these might be and who might need them. In any case, it seemed churlish to say no, so Firenza assented, but only if they were very desperate, which when given a second thought, meant only when things got out of hand, or did not go to plan, or had gone horribly wrong. But she was a straightforward kind of person, so she did not go back on the tentative agreement. Address details were duly given, though Firenza had the sneaking suspicion Lulu already had them and they made to leave.

"Just one thing," said Lulu as they pulled on their rain gear. "The Chinese delegation I mentioned are already here. In view of the information you have, and your recent travels, I advise you to be wary."

"What should we do?" Matters were now a great deal more ominous.

"Just be mindful of the situation. The Chinese are in town. There will be secret police everywhere. Stay home and know who your friends are."

Firenza left the meeting with a heavier weight on her head than when she went in. Outside the rain had turned from pouring to stair-rods. It was coming down so hard that there was not a gap in-between water drops. So fast and so torrential that the gutters could not deal with it. Great pools were forming across the street, getting wider by the minute and joining with other huge pools so quickly that they could barely cross the street before it became a lake.

"Best get home quickly," said Margot, pulling out another layer of rain gear to wrap around her shoulders. Firenza did the same. This kind of rain went through everything; welded rubber, plastic, PVC, laminates… sometimes you just could not have enough layers.

At the underground station, a man in a bright yellow sou'wester waved them hurriedly along. "Last train leaves in a few minutes. The buses have already stopped."

They ran quickly down the stairs. "Storm surge coming as well, be careful, Margot." And they ran to their separate platforms just as the security gates at the entrance to the station closed.

The tube compartment was filled with soaking travellers pooling water onto the floor. "What time is the surge?" she asked the bedraggled man standing next to her.

"About eight tonight."

She checked the time on the wall. It was three and already the city was shutting down. She messaged her work to say she would be going straight home after her lunch break due to the weather.

Weather. Weather was supposed to be a day-to-day fluctuation of dismal forecasts. They looked forward to when the sun broke through, even for a few minutes, but otherwise, it resembled a line of waterproof clothes stretching to infinity.

Passengers getting off the train wished each other good luck, and when Firenza eventually made it to street level she knew they would all need it. Ground floor dwellings were being hastily boarded up and storm-proof shutters raised. Sandbags were everywhere. The great steel barriers at the end of some streets were being raised, not to keep the water out, but to slow its progress and minimise damage. Firenza was glad she was living on the upper floor, but for the first time wondered if it was high enough.

She crashed through the puddles at speed. Her flat might be on the first floor, but the entrance was on the ground floor. She banged against the metal shutters which were already down, panic rising she fumbled for her mobile and hunched over it to try and keep it dry whilst she rang her neighbour.

"It's Firenza, I'm outside! Let me in!"

The storm-shutter groaned upwards and Firenza ducked underneath before it had lifted fully. The key fob which let her into the building slipped out of her wet hands. The shutter started its laborious journey back down, trapping her in a small dark space between it and the old wooden door. She groped for the fob and caught it just before it was washed out of the doorway into the growing flood outside, and fell into the hallway.

That was a close thing. Death by suffocation, death by drowning, death by screaming yourself inside out, the calm of the stairwell brought instant relief.

Shaking off her outer cloak, she saw a figure sitting on the stair.

"Tom?"

"I couldn't get out in time, so I came here. I still have a key to the flat but thought it best not to use it, you know, improper, or invasion, or something too threatening."

Dear Tom, it was nice to see him. Nice to have company on a night like this. She smiled. Of course, it was all right and she shook off her raingear just as the sirens of the city began their eerie wail. The Thames barrage was going up and the best they could all do was hope.

Chapter 14
The Nun

She had decided, in her own head, to become a nun at a very young age. It was not the result of some deep personal loss, as is sometimes the case, or even a family tradition, but a simple vocational calling. Her family had a moderate income, at least for Tibetans. In the West, they might be considered poor, but the West measures differently. The West measures in material goods and personal consumption. Not so in Tibet. In Tibet, if you could eat well, clothe your family and educate them, provide for your elderly relatives and smile heartily with your neighbours, you were considered fortunate. Most Tibetans were fortunate in this way.

Her most profound wish was that she could be allowed to study the cosmic order of things through the teachings of the Buddha and her family, touched by her apparent devotion to this area of study, felt it would be an honour for their eldest daughter to enter a nunnery. She was seventeen years old and embarking on a path none of her kin had travelled before.

As her sister nuns shaved her head for the first time, she felt her focus turn inward. No longer would her world be concerned with outward appearances. It was a relief, for now on she could devote herself to learning. Deeply grateful that she could be a nun. Her vows were her only possession, more precious than her own eyes, and she set about her daily life of manual labour and study of the Dharma.

The quiet girl became an even quieter nun. Although small in stature, she relished the manual work. Finding joy in the construction of stone walls, lightness of heart in the weeding and hoeing of the nunnery gardens, and gentle companionship in her sister nuns. The teaching was slow and defined, the meditation a challenge, but it was the life she had dedicated herself to and it was good.

If Tibet had been left alone to continue along its own path of development, Youngten would have grown within her monastic order and become enriched with symbolic empowerments and inner calm. Her name would have changed and, in her quest for enlightenment, she would be afforded spiritual protection on a higher level, along with those other nuns who were acknowledged as a fully realised being.

But distant and modest though her nunnery was, the rumbling in the grapevine had passed between monastery and nun, monk and mountain, of what the Chinese could do to remote Buddhist temples, and when a Chinese official came wandering up the hill with an escort of six guards and asked for an inventory of everything in the nunnery, they felt their time of peace was coming to an end.

Several months after this, a sizeable group of soldiers appeared at the foot of the rocky hill on which the nunnery was built. The little village built around the nunnery went into silent panic. Mothers and men collected their children and ran to hide. The soldiers marched stolidly upwards, inscrutable intent set upon their faces, guns and weapons across their shoulders. The nuns hastily gathered to decide what to do. They had heard the stories of nuns being shipped off to China for 're-education', of lifelong pacifists being forced to kill their animals, and stories of cruelty so frightening they could barely understand they were possible. Of only one thing, could they be sure; there was no love or compassion in the Chinese army. They felt hopelessly powerless.

It was a clash of civilisations. One unarmed and at peace. The other armed and belligerent.

The nuns felt they should not let the Chinese walk in and take over the nunnery without protest. They deduced that whatever way they tried to protect themselves, or whether they protected themselves at all, the result would go badly for them. So, they closed the gates under the entrance arch and attempted to establish dialogue from the topmost walls with their scant words of Chinese language pooled between them.

It did not go well.

The nunnery was never built as a fortified structure. The walls and gates were more to keep animals in, and sometimes out. Closing the colourful wooden doors in the walls was more to give a feeling of security, to prevent unnecessary surprises. The entrance gates were forcibly demolished in minutes and the nuns rounded up from their hiding places at gunpoint. Youngten noticed that not all were present, and desperately hoped some might escape, or at least stay hidden until the danger passed.

They were stripped of all their clothes and herded outside. Anyone protesting was shot, sometimes in the arm, sometimes in the leg. They were forced to watch the agony of the wounded. Anyone who went to help was also shot, but not killed.

They stood naked and shivering in the chilly mountain air, huddled together for security and modesty, whilst some soldiers went into the buildings and carried out anything which they considered to be of value. They did not take the beloved embroidered thangkas which had taken many months over many generations to make. They did not take the ancient books or the beautiful pictures. At first, this was considered good, then a small fire was lit in the corner of the old wooden building. They wept. Some had lived in this place for sixty years and ran to put the fire out with their bare bodies. Others, too scared to move, turned away, hiding their faces from this incomprehensible force of darkness.

The soldiers laughed and joked as the flames took hold, and one by one the naked women were thrown into the flames, even the wounded. The others were made to wait until the screams stopped before another was selected. A soldier walked up to Youngten and roughly pulled her round so that he could see her body. It was shameful beyond endurance. She begged for the flames, she tried to run for the flames, she doubled up to try and hide her pathetic little body from such cruel and malicious scrutiny. He laughed at her.

She was nineteen. A virgin. She had almost no knowledge of sex and little more of the principles of procreation. This was not where a nun's interests lay, so everything from then on was a horror of magnitude no nightmare could conjure, made worse because she could simultaneously see what was happening to the other younger nuns.

He punched her in the stomach and she doubled over. Then he forced her shocked body to its knees. She was slightly built, unprepared, and could not have resisted any part of what was to follow. She was winded from the stomach punch and could not cry out. Tears were springing from her eyes and she could barely see. She could not see him unfastening his trousers, but she felt, oh she felt, such terrible pain as something large and rough entered her anus. She felt her body splitting open, she wanted to die; she thought she would die. And then it was pushed into her again and again and, somehow, she did not die, just the unbearable, unfathomable pain, more and more, worse and worse, and she could not get away.

Uncomprehending, she whispered her mantra over and over, unable to process the pain, or the situation, or the motivation, and the pushing and shoving drove viciously into her body until she thought she was torn into pieces, and then when it stopped for a moment something hit her sharply on the side of her head and there was blessed darkness.

Her next memory was of being dragged roughly over stones. "Youngten, we have to go. You have to wake up. Youngten. Youngten." The voice was quiet but insistent and filtered through her subconscious. She assumed this was part of death, but the pain in her behind crept back, and the dragging was rough, and she could see another woman in front of her. She could see her bare arms being stretched, hands pulling on hers. She could feel the desperation in the other woman's voice. "Youngten, don't make me leave you here. Wake up or we both will die."

So, it wasn't death. It was disappointing. She was not properly prepared for death and, though it had seemed the least bad option for her, she realised it wasn't her time.

"Ahhhh," was all the noise she could muster as the stones ground into her chest. The pulling stopped and Youngten could see the other nun was naked as well.

"We have to hide quickly or they will find us," and her sister nun grabbed at some clothing strewn on the ground.

It was night. Youngten felt an outpouring of gratitude. She could not be seen and she could not see herself. She tried to sit but the agony was a cruel reminder of what has happened. She wanted to cover herself, but there was nothing. Just two small naked nuns cowering under a rough woven cloth, in a depression in the ground, terrified.

"Don't cry, don't cry, don't let them hear you."

Youngten stifled her sobs.

"They will not stay. We will go back in maybe two days."

The other nun was a little older, a little calmer, a little more worldly. In such times a little is a lot, and Youngten clung to her like a child, and they lay in a hollow, wrapped around each other, arms and legs entwined, blood on blood, sticky, drying, mingling.

The older nun stroked Youngten's hair and they slept to escape.

The sun rose, bringing warmth to their shivering bodies. The wind drifted past the burned-out nunnery and into their nostrils. Wakefulness brought pain and memory quickly to the fore.

Aware that they had neither bled to death nor frozen, they dragged each other to the nearby stream and lay in the needling cold to clean their wounds, their bodies, their spirits. Then they lay in the sun pulling branches and leaves over themselves for disguise. All was silent save the honking croak of the small band of Tibetan Eared Pheasants who lived near the nunnery, no doubt wondering where their breakfast was.

A shot.

The nuns jumped.

Then another, and another. They heard the fluttering of feathered wings and the honking alarm of the birds and held on to each other in fresh dismay and grief. Many generations of these birds had lived by the nunnery, had been fed by the nunnery and had lived as good neighbours with the nuns. They were completely tame. Without a shred of fear in their little bodies for humans, their trust had betrayed them. They would have almost walked onto the bullets.

Having roasted the birds on the smouldering embers of the monastic building, the soldiers did eventually leave, but it was another day and night before Youngten and her saviour dared to crawl up the slope.

There was almost nothing left.

They dressed in what they could find and limped and dragged themselves to the village at the foot of the hill, where local farmers took them in, hid them, fed them, mourned with them. It was a tragedy for all and a tragedy replicated across Eastern Tibet too many times.

Time passed and physical wounds healed. One young nun resolved to leave Tibet and join their spiritual leader, the Dalai Lama, across the mountains, across Nepal, and into his temporary home in India.

She did not understand the risks and they did not much care what those risks could be. The journey would turn out to be a long road of months stretching into years, but it was the only purpose they had.

Chapter 15
The Torrent

Firenza sensed it. The water on every side. Down the river, up the river. In the air, the sea, the river, the rain coming up through the drains. She sensed something calamitous.

General Li Enlai was in town. His presence added to her heightened sense of foreboding and visions of the burning monk, never far from her mind, stole into her inner sight.

A burning monk, a burning planet. Firenza shuddered. The brooding, culpable mood of the City of London and its embattled residents, long denied the truth about rising sea levels, was a sitting duck. It was fortunate that her modest flat was on a slight incline. More fortunate still that she lived on the first floor.

She and Tom stood together by the window. They were not far from the river and it was rising. The street lights reflected in its troubled swirl illuminated the bulging surface ominously. The rain came down in sheets, relentless, deafening. Far away in the estuary, the wheels of the barrage turned and the great steel barriers rose. Few understood the fact that the amount of water coming down the Thames was likely to be at least equal to the amount of tidal surge coming up, and this expensively enhanced feat of underwater engineering was about to be tested beyond its limits.

"We'd better get the people from downstairs," said Firenza. "They'll be scared stiff."

In the hallway, the unstoppable water was already seeping under and around the door. Firenza and Tom splashed through the tiled hallway, banging on the doors of the two flats below them.

"Come upstairs with us!" shouted Tom through the letterbox. The ashen face of Mr Keen appeared, his little dog, Poopsie, in his arms. He was all dishevelled in a worn dressing gown and slippers and horn-rimmed glasses.

"Very kind of you." He bowed slightly as he came out. Already Tom could see his slippers were wet. "Thought it would be bad, but this is worse than bad," said Mr Keen, and he gingerly picked his way through the deepening wetness on the black and white hall tiles.

At the other door, Ellen Pascoe was grumping obscenities at the weather. She grabbed a bag and stuffed her overly hairy cat into her bosom-filled cardigan for safe keeping.

"Blimmin' weather. Shouldn't be this bad, not at this time of year. Blimmin' forecast. Don't know what they are talking about. Heavy rain? You call this heavy rain? More like something Noah had coming. At least he was prepared. Blimmin' government. Don't know their arse from their tits. Come on, Wonker, let's go upstairs." And she continued muttering as she hauled her amply proportioned frame up the stairs.

In the upstairs flat all four stood silently and looked out the window in wonder and dread. They could hear nothing but the relentless slam of rain pelting on glass. The high and hulking sight of an industrial barge, torn from its moorings, loomed into sight. It careered lumpenly across their view and disappeared quickly downstream. Wonker risked looking out through the two unbuttoned windows of Mrs Pascoe's cardigan, caught sight of Poopsie and froze. Poopsie, for his part, was mesmerised by the scent coming from the general direction of the food cupboard and didn't notice, immediate investigations being called for.

Firenza looked amusingly from Wonker to Poopsie. Wonker and Poopsie — you couldn't make it up.

It was six o'clock, and still it rained, and the sirens wailed, and still the water rose. High tide was at eight and already the river had topped its banks in several places.

A building near the river crumpled and vanished. The watchers could not see the panic nor hear the screams, but they had enough imagination to understand the horror. Not everybody would escape with their lives.

Tom, good, decent, quiet and dependable Tom, left the depressing sight at the window and made a pot of tea in thoughtful silence. Shortly afterwards the city flickered helplessly into crashing darkness.

The Chinese Embassy in London was not far from Westminster Bridge, on a prime slice of real estate within spitting distance of the Palace of Westminster. General Li Enlai was booked into the suite reserved for high-level Chinese visitors in the nearby Hilton Hotel. It had been a long journey from Tibet, via Beijing, to London and he found he could do everything in the hotel except smoke. He called the number he had been given which promised 'Exceptional Services' and booked himself the promised pleasure for later that evening. Male or female, it wouldn't matter much to him.

He noted the rain and idly wished there could be more of it in China where water shortages were causing all manner of unrest. Not that he cared particularly. It wasn't his area of control and if a few people died of starvation when the harvests failed, it was of no interest to him. He was a soldier. He had respect. He would be fed. He ruled the system which had made him.

Li Enlai pulled on a raincoat, took an umbrella from the hotel lobby and resolved to go in the general direction of the River Thames for a quiet smoke. The doorman advised him not to stay out for long, but he didn't listen, didn't care, and barely understood English anyway.

Cosseted as he was in self-congratulatory thoughts of his new position as head of the training exchange between British and Chinese troops, General Li did not notice or understand that the city was quickly emptying. He did not know that it was peculiarly dark for the time of day and he did not understand how unusual this particular rain actually was. The weather forecast had not been in Chinese and he had not watched it anyway. What was a bit of weather to an important soldier like him?

After a while, he had the feeling he might be being followed. He turned round and the figure of a diminutive woman paused. Yes, he was being followed. He wondered why.

His shiny brown boots were getting wet, but it was of little concern to him. He had other pairs and the hotel staff would clean and polish these up like new anyway. Servants. He always had servants in one form or another. Sometimes he paid for them, sometimes it was indentured servitude, sometimes it was the government who supplied. However, they came into his employ, he would treat them as he liked. If they did not please him with a look or deed, he would punish them with gusto. Starvation, beatings, confinement, he really didn't think about it too much. Sometimes he locked them away and forgot about them. No one challenged him, ever. If they died, too bad.

He only got his hands dirty when it counted. Breaking the will of prisoners was his first priority. He did not care why it should be done, only that it should be done. As far as he was concerned, all Tibetans were enemies of the People's Republic of China, particularly the religious ones. It was personal. They were barely human and should be made to suffer. No one in authority had stopped him acting out his vengeful acts of cruelty and he believed he was on the high moral ground. Yes, he was on the front line protecting his country and, judging by the lines of medals on his chest, his country was conspicuously grateful. He smiled a smug, self-satisfied smile as he walked past the notable institutions of the defunct British Empire. Houses of Parliament, Big Ben, Westminster Abbey. All very grand in their way, but frankly pitiful in the face of Chinese economic dominance and his own great success.

He looked around, but the person tailing him was not there. He knew it was not his imagination, but shoved the idea away.

He would have liked to have tracked that errant monk down before he left his last post in dismal Tibet — the monk who had defied all attempts to be broken, who he had been told had escaped death outside the prison, and who his soldiers were at this minute tracking. It would be so nice to see him dead and tie up that last loose end. Funny, he mused, how some people died under the slightest pressure, and others endured to the last. It never ceased to stop entertaining him. He broke them all in the end, all, except for this one. Yes, he remembered that calm and peaceful face looking at him, silently begging for the electric shocks to stop. He remembered the monk's body shaking violently, sometimes for days, yet still that calm face looked straight at him. It had been almost a matter of personal pride to break the will of this one small man.

They all snapped in the end. Mental and physical wrecks, the dross of humanity, their broken bodies thrown out on the street to be a lesson for all. Except this monk. Thrown out for dead, yet somehow survived. He should have killed him with his own hands, but that would have been cheating. The enemies of the people had to be made to suffer. The general particularly enjoyed the freezing water treatment. He enjoyed watching as the bodies, hung by their feet, shook uncontrollably, and just when the shaking stopped, he would instruct the next bucket to be thrown. It was important they did not actually die of hypothermia. It was important they lived long enough to experience the dread of it happening again. Sometimes the men got erections in fright. That always made him laugh out loud. The cynical, rasping guttural laugh, born of cruelty, not humour. The laugh where the eyes do not smile; where the lips pull sideways to bare teeth, not mirth. The passionless laugh of the worst of humanity, the compulsive sadist.

As he turned to walk alongside the Thames, he caught sight of that small woman again and fancied she had her attention completely on him. Up ahead a car splashed to the kerb and parked a few yards away. General Li resolved to walk in a different direction. He did not hear the slam of the car doors above the sound of the rain. The reflections of the street lights danced their impressionistic sprites across the water and three rain-soaked people spread out in a fan around him. It was their chosen moment. They slowly closed in on the general — hands, on weapons, weapons under raincoats, fingers on triggers.

General Li heard distant sirens. It was the flood warnings, but his self-satisfied thoughts took no notice. Chinese factories used sirens to inform the workers when it was time to go home. He had fought a few battles, killed a few people, driven many to madness, and remained personally unscathed. He did not know humility or doubt. Those sirens were not for him.

As he walked through the deserted Millbank, coddled by the enveloping hubris of his invincible self, he noticed too late that the water through which he splashed was now almost ankle deep. He did not realise that the already flooded Victoria Gardens was not, in fact, the River Thames. As if shaken from a stupor he noticed the rain, harder, wetter, noisier. Maybe it was not just the rain. Only when it was blindingly obvious did he grasp that the river might have broken its banks.

He quickly changed direction, but an arc of assassins barred his way. They closed in on him and he felt fear for the first time. It ran into his spine, cold and clammy. Death, fickle, beckoned a crabby finger. Death to go forwards. His face paled. He turned to the black water.

Past the ankles, past the knees, the cold muddy water swirled, amassing increasing power with every second. He tried to retrace his steps back towards the hotel. Inside a minute he could not keep his footing. Panic rose. He had never experienced panic. At least panic was something he had learned to overcome as a small child, alone and cold, crying himself to distraction waiting for his mother who never came, that day, when the other children teased him for being a cry-baby. They did not let him forget it. For years he was branded the cry-baby, yet he would show them. He would never see his mother again, but he showed them all who was strongest in the end. A budding career in torture and cruelty was born outside those school gates. There, too, mercy had been buried.

The water asserted its strength with renewed vigour. Li's feet squished around inside his boots. He turned round to look back and those three determined shapes closed in on him. They had slightly higher ground and were herding him slowly, decisively, to the water. Soaking trousers stuck to his legs, the umbrella made its escape and was blown away, skipping across the flood in absurd freedom, while the blackness of inevitability shrouded his every thought. He was walking like a blind man, arms outstretched for balance, rain soaking into his coat, oozing straight out again, legs akimbo.

Li Enlai could not comprehend that he had lost control of the situation. His eyes searched everywhere for help, a lifeline, anything. It was beyond his mental powers to deal with any circumstance over which he had absolutely no power. Bewildered, he lost his footing. In a rush of confusion, he splashed to his knees in search of something to hold on to, to steady him, to break this unfathomable sense of being carried away by a force greater than himself. It happened so quickly that he hardly had time to forgive himself the oversight of not addressing his impending peril with military precision. The force of the icy water bowled him over like a tin soldier and he grabbed some railings to save himself from being swept away. He could weather this inconvenience. Luckily there was no one around to see him floundering and he felt his pride might still be intact. He was grateful his three pursuers were not in sight. The public spectacle of a Chinese general on his knees in a torrent of muddy water was not something he could endure. He tried to use the railings to haul himself upright. It was the wrong move.

The murky torrent rose several inches in a matter of seconds. It gurgled at him, swooshing and sloshing as it felt for the easiest route. It gathered pace anew, and swirled around and about the riverside seating, the trees, the walls. Uprooting, spinning, gathering all the detritus of London town as it went. Anything which moved was caught in the heaving current. Bags of rubbish, bins, traffic signs, animals, branches and bikes quickly pinned him to the railings. His arms and legs were forced through the gaps, breaking backwards at the joints and he screamed like a girl as the rising, ferocious deluge of tree and brick and sewerage piled over his gaping eyes, blinding him, choking him, damming his breath as it ripped him apart.

Margot, Bill and Lulu quickly left the scene, satisfied that justice had been done. Death by water. A fitting symmetry. Poetic almost.

His body would not be found. He would barely be a mention in the upper echelons of Chinese military society. They had always wondered how best to be rid of this particularly nasty sadist.

London would never be the same again. The flood of 2030 marked the beginning of the Great Exodus. The Thames Barrier had failed to protect the city. That which could be saved, was, but the ruins of splendid architectural achievements on either side of the riverbank were a sorry sight. Three hundred thousand buildings were flooded or destroyed that night, many of them homes. Fifty-one railway stations were rendered useless and thirty-five underground stations unsalvageable. One thousand electricity substations, four hundred schools and sixteen hospitals were knocked out of action. Four thousand people died and almost as many were unaccounted for. Some fine Georgian buildings were doomed to demolition and the wishful thinking of modern architects, who had substituted style for substance, paid the price in a thousand acres of splintered glass. The Palace of Westminster was a shoddy sight of crumpled stone and uprooted trees, a victim of its own inglorious excess and one of the first large scale sacrifices to the monument of consumer-driven climate change.

In the morning, Firenza and Tom went downstairs with their neighbours to survey the damage. It was first light and no one had slept. Some of the water had already drained away, but the splodgy lumps of stinking mud and sewerage stood for more than a quick clean. They opened the storm door and surveyed the scene outside. The half-naked body of a woman was unceremoniously propped against the steel barrier at the end of the street, one arm languorously wrapped across the top of it, head gently bent to one side, as if in repose. Like many others, she had not made it home in time. People stood helplessly in untidy clumps. No one seemed to know what to do with her.

It was still raining, but not so hard. Neighbours were already dragging their sodden furniture out onto the street. The scrape of shovel on floor echoed throughout the melancholy city and the River Thames gurgled and spewed its way to the sea carrying yet more flood water, unceremoniously gathered from the ongoing deluge two hundred and fifteen miles upstream.

There was no way out of the city. The roads were blocked with detritus and public transport was decimated. The next high tide would be in about two hours. Was it going to be worth saving anything except yourself?

Chapter 16
Ghurkas

Hunger woke them as the sun went down and the diminished band of travellers shared out their flatbread and dried yak cheese. It would do no good to talk about their losses. Losing valuable strength in mourning would not help them through the next gruelling days. It was best to be stoical.

They broke camp and trudged down the rocky slope Jampa had mapped out the day before. They felt safest amongst the towering boulders and talked a little about what Nepal might be like. Steeped in unhappiness, but well-fed, they could not have been less prepared for what lay in wait.

Rounding a particularly high bluff, they were met with an alarming sight. A small detachment of the Chinese People's Liberation Army, cosily dressed in expensive down jackets and snow boots, their rifles pointed directly at the Tibetans. The soldiers were mounted on great horned yaks, whose shaggy grey fur was lumpenly frozen and hung in tatters almost to the ground.

It was a shocking, gasping sight. Yaks were domesticated farm animals. They gave delicious fatty milk, meat and furs. To see such precious animals used as a war machine was, to the Tibetans, as surprising as it was frightening. Then the stupefying click as guns were cocked.

The Tibetans rushed to put their hands in the air — not that it was expected to make any difference. Their faces pleaded for their lives in horrified silence. Not one of them expected to live a minute more.

Yet the minutes were kind. From across the plateau, they could hear shouts. It was hard to know if this was friend or foe, but it was coming from a friendly direction. The approximate direction in which lay the biggest mountain in Nepal.

The army captain, if that was his rank, uttered something in guttural Chinese and waved his gun at them.

They fell facedown into the snow, assuming that was what he wanted them to do, feeling this could be the last action in their lives.

The shouts from below increased in volume as they echoed off the rocks behind. It was not Chinese. It sounded to Tashi like Ghurka. He hoped it was Ghurka. He prayed with every fibre of his body that it was Ghurka. The Ghurkas were long-time friends of Tibetans heading for exile. There were stories of Ghurkas guiding refugees over the mountains to safety. He squashed his eyes closed and prayed in his head that they would not be murdered just as they were about to be saved.

The six mounted Chinese weighed up the situation. They were not permitted to fight in Nepal and the border was very close. They may even have transgressed it. Their plan to have some fun with the struggling Tibetans was about to be thwarted, but they must save face and not leave empty-handed.

Jumping down from his surly mount, their leader jabbed the small nun with his rifle. She tucked her head tight into her chest, praying for invisibility in the snow. He pulled at her arm and dragged her upright. She was so light that he pulled her up and off her feet.

Tashi, Sonam and Jetsun, paralysed by fear, did not understand the situation quickly enough, but Tenzin scrambled to stand in front of her and was punched in the face with the sharp end of a rifle. He fell backwards, bleeding, a surprised look on this face.

The little nun shook uncontrollably. It could not happen again. She could not go with them. She had not walked and suffered this awful journey only to have a repeat performance of the depravity shown to her at the nunnery. The very thing she was escaping had caught up with her. The peace she so earnestly needed, almost within reach, was being barred to her. She cried out and fell to her knees, begging death.

The lead soldier grabbed the nun roughly by the neck and dragged her onto his yak. She fought with all the pathetic strength she had left, arms, legs, fists, feet, she would rather die than succumb. It was a brave show and a hopeless one. One punch to the head and she was unconscious.

The lumbering beasts turned back to the mountain. Lowing loudly in reluctance as they were prodded into action. A bunch of purple flowers named Violet Care wilted in the harness of the lead yak.

The Tibetans were stunned and shocked, powerless and shamed. They crouched on their knees to see, and maybe understand, the events which had so cruelly overtaken them. The little nun was being taken away to a fate almost all of them had some grasp of, but their impotence forced inaction. If they had had weapons, they might have used them to defend her, but there again, they were Tibetans and even wild anger was not an excuse to kill. Some of them floundered out of the snow and started to run after the yaks in the hope of retrieving the nun, but heavy shouts from the Ghurka people rushing up the mountainside implored them to stay down. They gesticulated wildly, heedless of their own danger, even as a few badly aimed parting shots settled the matter. What did it matter to the soldiers whether a few more Tibetans were injured or killed?

It was only luck that had brought the Ghurka people to this place, for it was not the usual route for a flight of refugees. Their village was not far away by Himalayan standards, but it was still another day's trudge.

With sadness and kindness, the robust people of the mountains took the bags of the travellers and shouldered the weight. They pressed clean cloth into the wounds in Tenzin's face.

"Good scar," said Tashi to Tenzin as the blood oozed thickly from his nose. He pointed to his own facial scars. "Not as good as mine!" They tried to laugh, but it was awful.

After a little food and drink, the Ghurkas offered their homes and their guides and together the two mountain peoples cried in relief and consternation. The Ghurkas knew the story of the Tibetans well. They knew about the suffering and the pain of their callous occupation and were it not for the inhospitable mass of mountains between Tibet and Nepal, they might have shared the same fate. Language understanding may have been sketchy, but the intent was well read. Their cultures were not so very different, nor were their everyday hardships. But one thing cut them apart. One nation was free, the other in chains of oppression.

Rested, the Ghurkas guided the dejected group of travellers down the mountainside. They had lost Karma and little Deyki, and now their Ana, the nun, would suffer unspeakable hardship and torture, all the more criminal because they later discovered that technically she had been abducted in Nepal. No one would take up her cause, because no one could. It was just a line in the snow and four insignificant Tibetans against the might of China.

Expertly guided, Tashi and the little band of refugees eventually made it through the remaining mountain passes to the Tibetan refugee camp in Nepal where they recovered their strength and were sent different ways according to the lists and quotas in the hands of the Nepalese government.

Tashi took out the amulet which his aunt had given him. It had remained hidden under his clothes for the entire journey, on a leather thong, round his neck. He offered it to the official managing his onward journey. "England," he said.

Chapter 17
Moving On

The mud, the terrible, sickening stench of death and decomposition within it made her retch.

All around, small committees of people were gathering to work out what best to do. Scratching their hats, shrugging their shoulders, nodding and shaking their heads in turn. Some stepped back from the group, some stepped forward. Ideas were exchanged and debated and inside the early hours of one morning, a community was born.

The young and strong went to help the elderly. A group of men volunteered to try and identify the dead woman languishing over the barrier at the end of the street and to get her to a morgue, or some transport, or whatever suitable conveyance came their way. In the event, they found more bodies and became the reluctant neighbourhood undertakers.

People set to work. Firenza and Tom were joined by others to sort out the ground floor flats of Ellen Pascoe and Mr Keen. They scraped and shovelled at the mud. There was no clean water to rinse out the rooms, so it was a case of brushing every last scrap out. Wooden furniture with a forever tell-tale timeline and watermark was stacked inside to dry, sodden upholstered chairs were dragged outside. The furniture looked as unhappy as the people.

The sky cleared a little and the rain eased a bit more. Someone gathered dry wood from somewhere and started a fire. Immediately a kettle was rushed to the scene and all over London a great and convivial connecting took place through the medium of a cup of tea.

Suddenly everything wasn't so bad. Everyone on the ground floor had pretty much lost everything, but everyone on dryer floors was preparing to donate what they had. Fortunately, the ratio of upper floors to ground floors was favourable and there was plenty to go around. There was mirth. No one knew where the next meal was coming from, but there was bonhomie, there was the barometer conveniently rising, and there was the good old British spirit making the best of things.

"I'm out of here," thought Firenza.

She stayed for a few days — just long enough to help the street clear up, if not dry up, and when Tom felt it was time to risk finding his way across the city, she packed a rucksack with food and a change of clothes. It was time for adventure. The sun was watery and she went outside to say some goodbyes.

A small mud-spattered figure stumbled untidily up the muddy street, a big smile on his face. He wore a maroon and saffron robe, and on his head was a tight woolly hat in red and yellow and white. Emblazoned across the edge, in black knitted writing, were the words 'Free Tibet'.

He walked up to the group Firenza was talking to, a wide and innocent smile across his lopsided face. Fingers pressed together, bowing profusely and grinning at the same time, he announced himself.

'I Tashi.' And he unpicked a violently crushed piece of paper that had been tucked into his wrap shirt. '10 Topping Street,' it said, 'Flat B.' He showed them the piece of paper proudly, then hurriedly put it back into his pocket for safekeeping, grinning even more broadly.

Firenza felt a bit stunned. The entire episode of the trip to Tibet and the subsequent intrigue had slipped her mind as the confusion of the flood, the tragic consequences for so many and her plan for the future rose in importance. She found the space in her brain allocated to the past and fumbled for more details as she mentally cobbled together the strained meeting with the human rights people at Bentinick Mansions with this physically scarred, but happy-looking monk.

"I stay here with you," he said in an accent so thick she could only just make out his meaning.

Firenza quickly stopped herself rolling her eyes. Here she was, on the veritable cusp of leaving for a brand-new life, when a house guest turns up.

"Cup of tea?" said Mr Keen, brandishing an enamel mug of the piping hot stuff in the general direction of the monk who fortunately caught sight of it out of the corner of his good eye.

One look at the enamel mug was enough. London was about to relive the war. Firenza held onto her eyes as they were again on the brink of soaring skywards. She had relived the war several times over with her grandfather as they sat together watching copious amounts of Yesterday TV when she was little and the familiar refrains were creeping through with the older residents of the street as they cleaned up.

Firenza introduced Tashi to Mr Keen and the enamel mug changed hands with much smiling and bowing. They didn't have a lot in common, least of all a language, but there was something of a connection, spiritually, and they talked and gesticulated, tea spilling everywhere, about Nepal of all things, and dogs, and Buddhism.

But here was an idea. Firenza was understandably reluctant to change her plans. So much of her future beckoned from beyond the unknown. She was too young to buckle back down under the yoke of pointless work and even more pointless debt. She knew to stay in London would crush her burgeoning spirit. If Mr Keen would look out for the monk, she would leave her flat as planned, with him in it, then when the communication systems were up and running contact her journalist go-between, Isaac, to sort out the mortgage. He was resourceful and he had the contacts.

It was not the greatest of ideas, but it was the only one she had.

London was over. It was inevitable. They'd clean up what they could, but the government offices had relocated to the new communications buildings in Manchester as soon as they knew the Thames Barrier was unlikely to control many more floods. The jobs would drift away as the corporations either left the city or the country. Sea levels had risen just enough for everyone to finally grasp what climate change meant. It would be a while before such a perfect storm would reoccur, but not a lifetime.

Firenza shouldered her rucksack and set off for higher ground. The sickening mud gave way to shiny suburban streets, and traffic, and business as usual. She and Tom parted with a hug on the outskirts of Ealing.

Meadows. She needed meadows.

Acknowledgements

With everlasting thanks to my dear friends and family for their love and encouragement as I carve out the space to write and grow as an author. Particular gratitude goes to Veronica Thomas who read through the manuscript in double quick time, and whose comments and judgement are truly appreciated